S0-CLP-167

Other
Sammy and Brian Mysteries
by Ken Munro

The Quilted Message
The Bird in the Hand
Amish Justice
Jonathan's Journal
Doom Buggy
Fright Train
Creep Frog
The Number Game
The Tin Box
The Toy Factory
The Medallion's Secret
Secret Under the Floorboard
The Mysterious Guest House
Fire, Smoke, and Secrets
Fireball
Grandfather's Secret
The Mysterious Baseball Scorecard
The Cross Keys Caper

The Sammy and Brian Mysteries are available at special quantity discounts for sales promotion, fund-raisers, or educational uses. For details, write to:

Gaslight Publishers
1916 Barton Drive
Lancaster, PA 17603

Email: kemunro@comcast.net

THE BUGGY HEIST
(THE LOST CAPER)

A SAMMY & BRIAN MYSTERY #19

BY KEN MUNRO

GASLIGHT PUBLISHERS

The Buggy Heist
(The Lost Caper)

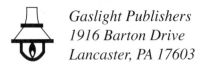

Gaslight Publishers
1916 Barton Drive
Lancaster, PA 17603

Email: kemunro@comcast.net

Library of Congress Number: 2007938170
International Standard Book Number: 978-1-60126-076-5

Printed 2007 by

Masthof Press
219 Mill Road
Morgantown, PA 19543-9516

DEDICATION

To the senior citizens who read
the Sammy and Brian Mysteries
before giving them to their
grandchildren.

Special thanks to:

Ron Munro
Gene Hansen
Tracy Palmer

"Please write one more."

Even though I intended to end the Sammy and Brian Mysteries, many fans insisted that I write one more. *The Buggy Heist* really is "the lost caper." It was to be Mystery #2. After I wrote the rough draft, I was not satisfied with the plot, so I filed it away and forgot about it. *Bird in the Hand* became book #2.

Feeling guilty that I let my fans down, I searched and found *The Buggy Heist* rough draft and brought it to life with a complete overhaul. I hope you find it to be the best of the Sammy and Brian series.

Since *The Buggy Heist* is a continuation of *The Quilted Message* and reveals the antagonist of the first book, you might want to read *The Quilted Message* first. That is not necessary, however, because *The Buggy Heist* is a self-contained mystery. This is true of each Sammy and Brian Mystery.

Enjoy the story!
Ken Munro

FOREWORD

From: Brian Helm (007½) < adrhelm@aol.com
To: < sammyw@comcast.net
Subject: RE: Hi, it's me.

Hi, Sammy,

Oh, boy, I'm working my first case out here in California. I went into Borders' Bookstore to buy a book. A man came up to me and asked if I wanted to buy a camera for twenty dollars. He said he wanted the money to buy a book. It was a digital camera. It looked great so I bought it. I also bought a book called *How to Avoid Con Artists*.

Here is the interesting part. When I went outside the store, I found a lady's pocketbook behind a potted plant and picked it up. After that, things got a little crazy. A woman and a policeman grabbed me and said I stole her purse. It was also her camera that I had in my hand.

My father paid my bail. I'm spending a lot of time in and around the bookstore, waiting for the man to return. The criminal always returns to the scene of the crime. Right, Sammy? When I catch him, I'll clear my name just like the time we were arrested. Do you remember the case, Sammy? You called it *The Buggy Heist.*

Always your best friend,
Brian Helm

CHAPTER ONE

The blue car lingered on the roadside for an hour. Its two occupants ignored the beauty of the surrounding rolling hills of farmland. Instead, their attention focused on the dirt lane that led from the farm.

Finally, a gray, horse-drawn, Amish buggy pulled out from the farm lane onto the narrow country road. Two Amish women and a grocery bag filled the buggy's front seat. The sharp, rhythmic sounds of the horse's hooves and metal-rimmed wheels on the paved road and the rustling of leather harnesses drifted over the nearby cornfields.

The tall, light-brown paper bag, crumpled from months of reuse, sat to the far right on the buggy seat. To the average observer, it was a bag of groceries. However, you don't take groceries to a bank.

The motor roared as the blue car pulled out and quickly came up behind the buggy.

"Showtime," the hairy-faced driver said to his female friend. He aimed the car's right front bumper at the buggy's rear wheel.

Sparks flew as the metal wheels scraped over the macadam. The Amish buggy fishtailed and skidded sideways onto the shoulder of the road. Skill and patience slowly brought the excited horse under control. As the dust settled, the blue car pulled ahead and parked in front of the carriage.

An Amish woman in her twenties stepped down from the buggy. She adjusted the black cap that covered her brown hair, parted in the middle and rolled back to form a bun. Her hands slapped at her simple, pastel green cotton dress, sending dust particles flying. She then turned to aid the other passenger from the carriage.

Gingerly stepping down was an Amish woman in her seventies. The black cap that concealed most of her gray hair and the thin black cape that protected her plain, lavender dress were sprinkled with debris. The older woman shook and patted away the loose dirt. Before she examined the damage, she blew the dust from her wire-rimmed glasses and re-adjusted them to her face.

The car door slammed, and the man ran toward the women. His bushy hair, black mustache, and bristly black beard contributed to a very hairy face. His red sweat suit did not relate to his solemn expression, nor did the gloves he wore match the warm July morning.

The stranger appeared friendly as he joined the women in the inspection for any damage. He expressed concern for their safety and seemed relieved that the women were not injured and no damage had occurred to the horse and buggy.

While the nervous Amish women were busily engaged in a business-like conversation with the man, the female snuck from the car to the opposite side of the carriage. Her long blond hair and heavy makeup showed signs of tension. The hair was losing its curl, and the runny makeup was creating a facial mudslide. The jogging suit she wore was over-sized and hung like excess body fat. Had the Amish women noticed her returning to the car, they would have wondered why a pregnant woman was wearing a jogging suit.

The hairy stranger abruptly excused himself and hurried to the car. The car sped off in a whirl of dust, leaving the women coughing and confused about his hasty departure.

"Did you get it?" the hairy man asked his female passenger.

She pulled up her sweatshirt and exposed the paper grocery bag containing $200,000.

CHAPTER TWO

At the same time . . .

Sammy Wilson and Brian Helm, Bird-in-Hand's fifteen-year-old amateur detectives tilted their bikes over on the grass.

"Bring your bikes back here," came a woman's voice from the side of the corner brick house. Red hair poked out from under her wide-rimmed garden hat that flopped about as she waved. Remnants of dirt flew away from the trowel she held. Large sunglasses on her round face added a mysterious air to the stout woman. Her ill-fitted jeans showed signs of habitual garden work.

Brian picked up his bike. "She must be the woman who called you yesterday."

"Must be," Sammy said, following Brian along the side yard to the back of the house.

The woman hurried to the back porch and flopped down on a wicker sofa. "Hi, I'm Mrs. Thomas. Come up here where we can talk in private."

The boys left their bikes on the grass and stepped up onto the porch.

"I'm Sammy Wilson. This is Brian Helm."

Mrs. Thomas smiled. "You come highly recommended." She pointed to two white wicker chairs. "Please sit down."

Sammy tried to "read" the person behind the sunglasses. All he knew for sure was that she was married to Frank and was a middle-aged woman with a problem. "You said on the phone that you're having a problem with your eighteen-year-old son."

"Yes, he's going into business with a friend. Both are putting up equal amounts of money."

Sammy waited. "And the problem?"

"We don't have any money, but William, that's my son, said that his father and I are not to worry, that he has the money for the partnership."

"He must be a smart boy," Brian said.

"Not really," Mrs. Thomas said. "He has a job at the Bird-in-Hand Family Restaurant, and he gets into these questionable money-making schemes. Heaven only knows where the extra money comes from."

"He won't tell you?" Brian asked.

"He's eighteen, independent, and keeps his secrets." Mrs. Thomas looked out over the flower gardens that enhanced the yard. She smiled and glanced back at the boys. "That's what most teenagers do. Right? They try to separate themselves from their parents." She lost her smile and added, "But it's hard to let go of your children. You want to protect them."

"You have us at a disadvantage," Sammy said. "You were a teenager, but we have not yet been parents."

The sunglasses hid any expression of grief. "Your time will come, but for now . . ."

"You want Brian and me to find the source of your son's money."

"Exactly. He works at The Bird-in-Hand Family Restaurant. You can start there. I'll make a list of my son's friends and other information that might help you."

"Do you have a picture of your son?"

"Not with me. I'll get it to you tomorrow, along with the list."

The young super sleuth hesitated. "I have to tell you that if your son is involved in any illegal activities, we will have to report it to the police."

Mrs. Thomas' right hand shot up to her mouth. "Oh, dear, really?"

In the speechless void that followed, an airplane flew overhead, a neighbor's dog barked, and a squirrel jumped from a tree limb to the roof of a storage shed.

"Oh, well, let's hope it doesn't come to that, but if you must, you must," she said.

Her sudden lack of compassion for her son caused Sammy and Brian to glance at each other.

Before they had a chance to comment, Mrs. Thomas reached for the thermos bottle and paper cups beside her. "I bet you boys are thirsty. How about some lemonade?" she asked.

CHAPTER THREE

As the boys entered the Bird-in-Hand Country Store, they encountered a dispute near Sammy's baseball card counter.

"Sammy, good, you're here," Mrs. Wilson said. "David Schultz wants his money back."

David was eighteen and a regular customer of the store. Sammy knew David Schultz from school as well as from his baseball card collecting, but he never knew David to be a hothead.

The boy stood face-to-face with Sammy. He twisted his baseball cap, reversing the bill to the back, enabling him to stand closer. "I'm going to give you one more chance before I cause some trouble here. This Nolan Ryan rookie card has a crease. It was bent when you sold it to me."

Sammy stood his ground and stayed calm. "We talked about this before. All I can do is repeat what I told you Saturday. The card was in that rigid, plastic sleeve. In fact, you took the card out of the sleeve and inspected it. The card was not bent at the time you bought it, or I'm sure you would have mentioned it."

"I didn't see the crease, but it was there," David said, trying to convince himself as well as Sammy.

Angie Lowe, a blond and David's girlfriend, shifted her packages from one hand to another and avoided eye contact. She apparently wanted no part of the argument and moved to the next room to inspect the Amish wall hangings.

"How long have you been collecting baseball cards?" Sammy asked, knowing that David was an avid collector.

"Seven years, but that's none of your business. I want my money back!"

"You apparently are a serious collector and know that the condition of a card can affect its value. As I remember, you took a long time inspecting the card." Sammy hated to be persistent, but he knew the Nolan Ryan card was not creased when he put it in the paper bag the previous Saturday.

"Well, when I got home and examined it again, I saw the crease," David said defiantly. "I don't buy damaged cards."

Sammy remembered that another boy was with David and Angie on Saturday. He decided to use another tactic. "After you left here Saturday, you showed the card to your friends, didn't you?"

"Yeah, so what?"

"Was the card taken out of the plastic sleeve once or twice?"

"Only once," David said defensively. Then seeing Sammy smile, he added, "Paul wanted to see it up close. Something wrong with that?"

Sammy scratched his head. "It's possible your friend bent the card when he tried to put it back into the sleeve."

David lowered his eyebrows. "He would have told me if he had."

Sammy looked David in the eye. "Would you say anything if you damaged something valuable without being seen?"

David's left eye twitched. "Hey, man, the card is bent. I want my money back."

"I can't do that," Sammy said reluctantly. He pointed. "See that sign? All sales are final."

Sammy's mother and father were standing nearby to assist their son if things got out of hand. The Wilsons lived upstairs above the shop. Sammy's mother had started the Bird-in-Hand Country Store as a hobby. The shop handled Amish-made quilts and antiques. It became so successful that Mr. Wilson quit his job to help run the store. Sammy was given space to display and sell his baseball cards. Now his parents were giving him space to develop and learn in this confrontation with an irate customer.

"This is a gyp joint," David said, reversing his cap. "I'll get you, Sammy. You just wait. Your time will come, man." He looked around for Angie but didn't see her. "Angie, come on. Let's get out of here."

Sammy stayed calm and followed David to the door. They both turned and saw Angie in the other room, descending the stairs that led to the Wilsons' living quarters.

"Sorry, I thought the upstairs was part of the shop," she said as David grabbed her hand and pulled her out the door.

Brian, who had taken refuge in the next room, had heard the argument between Sammy and David. He always felt uncomfortable in a negative environment. When bad things happened, he wanted no part of it.

"That was neat the way you got David to admit that someone had taken the card from its plastic sleeve after they left the shop."

Sammy shrugged. "I put him in a bind by giving him only two choices. Was the card taken out of the sleeve once or twice? No matter which choice he picked, he was admitting the card was taken from the protective sleeve. David picked the choice less incriminating."

"When he said, 'Only once,' you had him. Right, Sammy?" Brian's grin turned into a frown as he glanced out the front window. "Do you think David will cause any trouble?"

"No. He knows he or one of his friends bent the card," Sammy said, returning to the counter. "It's human nature to blame others for our own mistakes. Sometimes it's hard to face the truth."

Brian was proud to add, "Like at school. We blame the teacher when we don't get good grades. Right, Sammy?"

Sammy was deep in thought, trying to remember the last time he had received a bad grade. He was always interested in the world around him. That curiosity provided the motivation to search for answers. He asked questions, read books, magazines, newspapers, and observed. Sammy was not content to sit around watching television—watching other people earning their living while his precious time slipped away. He wanted to prepare for his own future. Watching his own experiences grow was more satisfying. At school, he headed the Brain Teasers Club, which allowed him to interact with his peers. He had many friends, but Brian was his very best friend.

Brian sat in the chair he considered his own in the main room of the shop. He slipped into his own world as Secret Agent Double-0h-Seven and a Half. He lifted the collar of his imaginary trench coat and squinted. He was anxious to start investigating Mrs. Thomas' son William. *Where was he getting that extra money?* Brian wondered.

Mrs. Wilson finished with a quilt customer and then directed a young girl to the restroom, located in the back room. Mr. Wilson manned the cash register, taking care of the quilt sale.

Four tourists entered the shop, followed by a teenager. Sammy recognized the thin, sandy-haired, nineteen-year-old as a high school dropout. George Burk visited the shop many times, looking for antiques. The last Sammy heard, George was trying to start an antique business in the area.

Two women tourists wandered into the small quilt room, containing a hundred quilts of varying colors and patterns. One man was drawn to Sammy's baseball card display. The other man inspected the quality of the Amish-made birdhouses.

George Burk appeared anxious as he approached Sammy. "Hey, where's your restroom?"

"Someone's in it right now," Sammy said, recalling a girl asking his mother for the restroom. "It's in the back room. She should be out soon."

"I really have to go," George said, his face straining.

"Well, okay," Sammy said, then motioned. "If it is an emergency, use our private bathroom up those upstairs in the next room. It's the first door on your left."

"I hope he makes it," Brian said, raising his eyebrows and clinching his teeth. Then changing the subject, Brian asked, "Do you think this week will be as exciting as the mystery we solved last week?"

They both looked at the Amish Album quilt hanging on the wall. *The Case of The Quilted Message*, Sammy had called it when he entered its details into his diary. Amos King, an Amish man, ran a successful woodworking shop. He sold his woodcrafts to tourists and local vendors. Not trusting banks, he hid his money without telling his wife where. "She talks sooner than her mind can think," Amos would say. He had no intentions of anyone knowing the location of his hidden money.

Amos had no children, and his money accumulated. Thinking that as he got older his memory might fade or he might die, he had a mysterious quilt made. The quilt contained twenty cloth pictures that were clues to the location of his money. Amos admired his wife for her skill at solving crossword puzzles. He knew she could solve the quilt's puzzle should anything happen to him. He left a message in his personal Bible with a reference to the reason for the quilt. Later, Amos King died in a fire that destroyed his woodshop. His money was never found. The note in his Bible went unread. Mrs. King donated the quilt and other things to the local fire company for their auction. Sammy's mother bought the quilt and hung it on the wall of her shop as a conversation piece.

When word got around that the quilt's pictures might contain information as to the location of Amos King's money, a break-in occurred at the shop. Sammy rescued the quilt in the scuffle with the intruder. Sammy and Brian, through trial and error, solved the quilt's message, but so did the persistent, mysterious intruder. With the help of their friend, Detective Ben Phillips, the boys set a trap and captured the guilty party.

"I wonder if the money is in the bank by now?" Brian asked, recalling the adventure of the previous week.

Sammy checked his watch. "Mary Fisher told me on Saturday that she was taking Mrs. King to the bank this morning. I'd say it was deposited about two hours ago."

"Thanks for the use of your restroom," George Burk said. He motioned to the old table windup phonograph with a horn on top. "How much you asking for the phonograph?"

"One hundred," Sammy said.

George shook his head. "I'll think about it."

Three teens came in the front door. One of the three newcomers recognized Sammy. "Hey, Sammy. Man, I didn't know you worked here."

Travis Wells was a seventeen-year-old who was trying to establish himself as a rock musician. His hair was shaved on the sides. The rest was sprayed to defy gravity, spiking the air above it. Sammy knew Travis from school and had enjoyed his band at social gatherings. He thought Travis had potential as an up-and-coming musician.

"My parents own the shop," Sammy said, looking at the trio. "How's the music business?"

"We're creating a new sound," said Travis. "We're getting away from hard rock. We're leaning more toward the plowed dirt sound. You know, man, rich and fertile. It's the Amish sound—hard working, domestic, toil and sweat. It's music that's stern and powerful, yet meek and peaceful."

Sammy tried to imagine the Amish sound, but gave up. His left-brain logic could not draw upon the musical knowledge of his right brain. *It would be an interesting experience to hear though,* he thought.

"Hey, this is Jenny Herr. She plays the keyboard," Travis said, pointing to a petite blond, slopping gum. "And this is my drummer, Mike Stiles."

"Hi," Sammy said.

Jenny stopped chewing and nodded her head. Mike drummed a couple of beats on the glass countertop with his hands.

Sammy pointed to Brian. "Do you remember Brian from school?"

Mike winked and snapped a finger. "Sure, Brian Helm. How you doin'?"

Brian nodded and half smiled. His mind was still muddled on the plowed dirt sound.

Travis panned the room. "We're looking for black Amish hats to wear on stage. You sell them here?"

"Right around the corner, in the next room," Sammy said. He smiled and added, "You'll have to cut holes in the hat or flatten your hair to assure a good fit."

"The spikes will go," Travis said. "Our next hair cut will be with a bowl over our heads."

Travis Wells stayed behind while Jenny and Mike went into the next room. He asked Sammy if he had heard his band play. When Sammy said yes, he asked his opinion of the music.

After Sammy gave him his evaluation, Travis bent closer to Sammy and whispered, "I want you to know I'm not one to hold a grudge." Without further comment, Travis joined the other two in the next room.

Brian looked at Sammy. Sammy looked at Brian but said nothing.

Brian shrugged. "Well, what was that all about?"

"A year ago, in school, after a basketball game, I saw Travis take money from another boy's locker. I reported it to the coach, and he suspended Travis from the team for two weeks. He found out later that I was the one who turned him in."

Brian gritted his teeth. "Then what did Travis do?"

"That's the strange part. He didn't do anything."

"He must be one of the few who doesn't blame others for his mistakes," Brian said and strolled back to the wooden chair in the corner. As he plopped down, he asked, "Hey, when do we start working our new case?"

Bruce Harris, a neighbor, stuck his head in the doorway. "Did you hear what happened? Two robbers crashed a car into Mrs. King's buggy and stole a bag full of money right from the buggy."

Sammy listened in disbelief. "Was anyone hurt?"

"I don't think so," Bruce Harris said. "The police have the car used in the holdup. It's up in the Farmer's Market parking lot. The police are up there now."

Mrs. Wilson hurried out from the quilt room. Mr. Wilson left the cash register and, with Sammy and Brian, ran out the door. They all glanced up the street toward the Farmer's Market, where the police were trying to disperse a crowd that had gathered.

Brian jumped up and down and waved his hands. "Oh, boy, we have another mystery to solve. We can forget Mrs. Thomas' problem for now. Right, Sammy?"

Sammy was thinking of Amos King. Even from the grave, he was preventing the bank from getting his money.

"Who would do this?" Mr. Wilson asked, leading the group back into the shop. "After the troubling times Mrs. King went through, I can't believe someone would steal her money."

Stunned and angry, Sammy was determined to focus his time and energy toward recovering the money. The robbery was now a police matter, but he felt an obligation. He would feel incomplete until the money was in the bank and Mrs. King had the financial security she deserved. He glanced at the quilt hanging on the wall.

"What are you thinking, Sammy?" Brian asked.

"I'm thinking that, this time, the quilt won't reveal the location of Amos King's money."

CHAPTER FOUR

"**M**om, Dad, I'm going out!" Sammy shouted as Brian and he headed for the door. "We're going to the parking lot to gather facts about the robbery."

"Okay, but try not to solve the case all in one day," Mr. Wilson joked.

The mid-day, July air got hotter as Brian tried to catch up to Sammy. That was Brian's world. He was always trying to catch up to his best friend. "Hey, let's walk. It's too hot to run."

"I have a hunch Detective Phillips will be in charge of this case," Sammy said over his shoulder. "If we hurry, we might catch him before he returns to the station."

The Farmer's Market was one block east of the Bird-in-Hand Country Store on Main Street. The presence of Channel 8's remote van and the police activity marked the spot of the abandoned blue car.

As the boys approached the marked off area, Detective Ben Phillips was walking away from a live interview with Janelle Stelson. The tall, heavyset detective with piercing eyes, a thin mustache, and a receding hairline presented a formidable figure.

Because of the friendly rapport and respect that had developed between the teenagers and the detective, Sammy was confident that Phillips would share details and clues of this case with them.

"Well, hello, Sammy and Brain," Detective Phillips said. "Duck under the tape, and we can talk. It looks like we have a chance to find Amos King's money again."

"Speaking of chance," Sammy said, "what's the chance that Lloyd Smedley is involved in this one, too? He's out on bail, isn't he?"

"Yes, he's out on bail, but no chance. According to the victims, Mary Fisher and Mrs. King, the robbery was done by a younger, hairy-faced man and a woman." He pointed to the blue car being inspected by the crime unit's forensic team. "This is the car they used."

"What can you tell us about the robbery?" Sammy asked.

"Can you believe Mrs. King still had the $200,000 in the grocery bag? Well, anyway, Mary Fisher was taking Mrs. King to the bank. The money was on the front seat of the buggy. The way they tell it, the car came from behind, grazing the rear wheel. They pulled the buggy over, got out, and inspected it for damage. According to Mary, a man with black bushy hair, a mustache, a beard, and wearing a red sweat suit left the car and spoke to them. A female must have been in the car and got out. Mary recalls seeing the back of a blond female getting back into the passenger side of the car. Evidently, the male kept the women's attention while his female partner went to the opposite side of the buggy and grabbed the money. The women didn't know the money was gone until they got back inside the buggy. By that time, the car was long gone."

Sammy combed his fingers back through his straight, black hair, revealing concerned blue eyes. "That black facial hair and that red sweat suit sound like disguises to me."

"You could be right," Ben Phillips said.

Sammy glanced around. "Where are Mary and Mrs. King now?"

"The women were pretty upset, but they didn't want any help. Mary took Mrs. King back to the farm. I told them I'd keep in touch."

Sammy looked for a shade tree as he wiped his brow with his arm. He smiled to himself. *Dumb,* he thought. *You don't usually find trees in the middle of a parking lot.*

Brian was inspecting the outside of the car. "Sammy, this car looks like Glen Clover's blue Nissan. Do you know who I mean?"

Sammy took a wide sweep around the opened door, bent down, and inspected the left front bumper.

Detective Phillips followed. "I'll be able to tell you boys the owner of the car when I hear back from the station," the detective said. "They're running a trace on the license now."

"You don't have to wait," Sammy said. "This is Glen Clover's car. Look here. See the crack in the headlight frame and this vertical dent in the bumper? Glen did that last winter when he slid into a light pole in the school's parking lot."

"Hey, Ben," called one of the lab men, standing by the open car door. "Look at this." He pointed to a long, blond hair, hanging from the doorframe on the passenger side. "Our suspect brushed her head across the door frame, leaving a single hair caught on a burr. We already have two strands of black hair found on the driver's seat. Oh, and don't count on fingerprints. They wore gloves."

"I sure would like to hear Glen Clover's side of this," Sammy said, trying to visualize Glen being involved in the robbery.

Detective Phillips motioned toward a white Chevrolet. "While we're waiting for the forensic team to finish up, let's jump into my car and go have a talk with Glen Clover."

"Do the police have air conditioning in their cars?" Sammy asked.

"You're reading my mind, Sammy," the detective said. "Why suffer here when we can travel in comfort?"

On the way, Detective Phillips called in to confirm the owner of the car and the address. The two boys had ridden in this car to catch and arrest Lloyd Smedley. Now, three days later, they found themselves in the same car, starting a new case. Sammy wondered whether Lloyd Smedley had his hands in this one.

Glen's mother answered the door and directed the trio to the building beside the house. Part of the garage had been converted into a woodworking shop. As they walked into the garage through the half-opened door, they saw Glen Clover sanding the lid of a pine box.

The lean, blond teenager, wearing a white T-shirt, jeans, and a sports cap, looked up and dropped his sander. "W-w-who are you?" he quivered to the six-foot-two, two-hundred-ten-pound detective staring down at him with dark penetrating eyes.

"Detective Phillips," the intimidating figure said as he showed his badge.

"You scared me," Glen said. "Are you here about the car?"

"Yes," Phillips coughed out as his lungs tried to reject the airborne sawdust. He stepped aside. "I believe you know Sammy Wilson and Brian Helm."

"Yeah, hi," Glen said and grabbed a shop towel to wipe the mixture of sweat and sawdust from his face. "Are you recovering stolen cars now, Sammy?"

Brian sneezed, walked over and picked up the sander, and placed it on the worktable. "Glen, you should have a sign on your garage."

"What? Glen's Woodworking Shop?" Glen asked.

Brian grinned. "No, a warning sign that says sawdust may be hazardous to your health."

Glen went around the visitors and pushed the doors open all the way. "I plan to put an exhaust fan in here soon." He slipped his sports cap off and slapped it against his left arm, adding more dust to the air.

The detective backed away. "Your car was found abandoned in the Farmer's Market parking lot."

"That's different," Glen said unconcerned. "The car is further away this time."

"What do you mean, *this time?*" Sammy asked.

"My car was stolen twice before. Each time, I found it the next day, parked two blocks away from here."

"So your car has been stolen three times?" Sammy asked.

Glen nodded. "Each time, it was taken from the driveway." He pointed to the pine box. "When I work on large projects in here, I need the room, so I park the car outside."

"Do you leave your keys in the car?" Sammy asked.

"No, that's the funny part," Glen said. "I don't know how they do it. It's a mystery to me. The car doors are locked. The only extra key is in the house."

"Were the wires under the dash tampered with?"

"No, so don't ask me how they do it," Glen said. "They just do it and take a joy ride."

"Somebody got a lot of joy out of your car this time," Brian said, moving closer to the open doorway and fresher air.

Glen Clover's matter-of-fact attitude changed to one of concern. "It wasn't damaged was it?"

"Your car was used in a robbery at nine this morning," Phillips said. "Where were you at that time?" his dark eyes zoomed in on Glen's blue-gray eyes and met little resistance.

"I . . . I was in bed," Glen stammered. "I got up at 9:00. I saw the car was gone, and I called the police. Hey, you don't think . . . I don't do that kind of stuff."

"Do any of your friends know about the extra key you keep in the house?" Detective Phillips asked.

"Not that I know of. The car was my father's. He gave it to me when he bought a new one. There was only one key, so I had a copy made. That's the one I keep in the house."

Sammy was in his element. Here was another puzzle to solve, a puzzle connected to the disappearance of Amos King's money. The car had been "borrowed" twice before, but not connected to a crime. *Why now?* Sammy wondered. *Are the same people involved this time?*

When they finished up with Glen Clover, Detective Phillips drove Sammy and Brian back to the country store. He returned to the station to update his reports, and the boys went directly to Sammy's bedroom.

The bedroom was to the right at the head of the stairs. It functioned more like a den with a bed. A heavy oak desk that had been Sammy's grandfather's supported a computer, printer, and scanner. Various maps covered one wall. Four puzzle-solving plaques awarded to "Samuel Wilson, the Puzzle King" hung on the opposite wall. His mother insisted they be displayed properly and not hidden away in a drawer. An orange and black Orioles' pennant and poster gave color to the same beige wall.

The other two bedroom walls Sammy valued the most, for they allowed him to travel beyond the room. The back wall was lined with wall-to-wall bookshelves, containing fiction and nonfiction books. The front wall provided two large windows that overlooked Bird-in-Hand's Main Street. From there, Sammy studied the faces and behavior of the people below—Amish, non-Amish locals, and tourists.

Under the simple pine bed and a bureau with scuffed and scratched surfaces were neatly arranged piles of *Newsweek, Time, Reader's Digest,* and puzzle solving magazines.

Brian flopped down at the foot of the bed, his usual ritual. He said he was comfortable there. Sammy theorized that his friend sat at the foot because he felt inferior to other people his age.

Sammy was deep in thought as he slipped his trim body into the wooden desk chair and activated the computer. He watched the screen as it came to life, maybe expecting it to reveal the robbers' identities. When reality set in, he knew the only way to catch the robbers was to use his other computer, his brain.

The impending silence caused Brian to fall back and scan the ceiling. After allowing his eyes to follow several cracks in the plaster, Brian asked, "Well, which case do we work first, Mrs. Thomas' or Mrs. King's?"

Sammy leaned back and locked his fingers behind his head. "I'm not anxious to find Mrs. Thomas' son involved in illegal activities, if he is. Besides, we don't have his picture or the list of his friends yet. At the moment, let's put our energy into investigating the robbery."

Brian sat up. "We can start by making a list of the people who knew that the money was going to the bank this morning."

"I was thinking the same thing."

"You were?" Brian said, producing a gratifying smile.

"Yep," Sammy said, "until I remembered the media mentioned that Mrs. King was taking the money to the bank Monday morning. That list of suspects would be a long one."

Brian frowned, then, wanting to redeem himself, said, "I say we start with Lloyd Smedley. He wanted to stay out of the picture this time, so he probably hired someone to do the job for him." Brian bounced off the bed. "Let's go. Detective Phillips said he's out on bail."

Sammy shot his hand out. "Now wait a minute, Brian. Let me call Detective Phillips. I'm sure he wants to interview Smedley, too. We can arrange to be at the station then."

"We'll interrogate him. Right, Sammy? You can use that bind thing. You say, 'Lloyd Smedley, did you steal the car or the money?' No matter which one he picks, you'll have him."

"The bind wouldn't work on Smedley, because he knows we can't prove that he has any connection to the car or the robbery. The first thing he'd say is, 'What car? What money?'"

Brian slipped into his secret agent mode. He stood tall and, in his deepest voice, said, "Then, I'll have to use my own world-renowned psychological technique."

"World renowned?"

"Yep, my famous 'Yes' interrogation technique."

"It sounds deep. How does it work?"

"I'll try to keep it simple so you understand. I look Smedley in the eye and say—"

"Which eye?" Sammy asked. "The right eye or the left eye?"

"It doesn't matter," Brian said. "Just pick one."

"If you stare between the two eyes, he'll think you're staring at both of them at the same time."

"I know that, but with the 'Yes' technique, you only need one eye."

"That's nice to know," Sammy said.

"So I say, 'Is your name Lloyd Smedley?' And he says, 'Yes.' And I say, 'Do you live on Poplar Road?' And he says, 'Yes.' And I say, 'Do you operate a flea market stand?' And he says, 'Yes.' And I say, 'Did you arrange for Mrs. King's money to be stolen yesterday?' And he says, 'Yes.'"

"Why will he say yes to that last question?"

"Because that's how it works. You use at least three questions that require a 'yes' answer. That sets up a 'yes' response for the next question. Then you slip in the incriminating question, and if it's true, he'll answer 'yes.'"

"Have you tried this technique before?" Sammy asked.

"Yes."

"Does it work on men or women?"

"Yes."

"And it always works?"

"Yes."

"And does it ever fail?"

Brian shook his head and said, "No."

"Brian, I'm afraid your world-renowned technique just came home and laid an egg."

Brian thought about the questions Sammy asked him and his answers. "Hey, I'll rework it. It just needs a little adjustment."

"While you're doing that, I'll call Detective Phillips to see if we can arrange a meeting with Lloyd Smedley."

As soon as Sammy was gone, Brian said, "Did Sammy leave the room? Yes. Am I testing out my super interrogation technique? Yes. Is Sammy calling Detective Ben Phillips? Yes. Did I make a fool of myself in front of Sammy? Yes."

Brian looked at the door and said, "It worked this time, Sammy."

CHAPTER FIVE

D etective Phillips had Lloyd Smedley in the interrogation room when Sammy and Brian arrived at the police station the next morning. Official questions concerning Smedley's potential involvement in the robbery had already been asked. He pleaded innocent of all allegations.

Now it was the boys' turn.

Sammy felt strange confronting the man he helped capture and who faced a ten-year jail term. The man before him was in his forties, his sandy hair combed slightly to the front. He had a face capable of playing many parts. In a movie, he could be the good guy, the bad guy, a friend of the good guy, even a lawyer or the town drunk. The last role he played in real life was that of a greedy, sneaky, scoundrel out to get Amos King's money.

The amateur detective looked at the weary man sitting on a wooden chair on the other side of a plain, wooden table. "Do you still blame me for your criminal actions?" Sammy asked.

Smedley concentrated on his folded hands on the table. "I'm disappointed in you, Sport. If you came looking for a revengeful man, you ain't going to find him here." His gray eyes looked up at Sammy. "I didn't steal no car, and I didn't steal the bag of money. I already told the detective here I don't know nothing about it."

"Maybe you didn't steal the car or the money, but you could have hired someone to do it," Sammy said.

Smedley's fist pounded on the table. "Yes, I could have, but I didn't." He hesitated and took a deep breath. He held his hands out in front of him, palms showing. "Look, I know what I done was wrong. I'm willing to spend jail time for it. Believe it or not, I don't blame you. Maybe you even done me a favor. Who knows?"

Sammy searched the man's eyes for any signs of truth. Last week's experience taught the super sleuth that this man could not be trusted. But what had last week's experience taught Smedley? Had he really changed? Was this a new Lloyd Smedley or the old Lloyd Smedley playing a new role? Sammy decided to give him the benefit of the doubt and asked, "Do you have any idea who could have stolen the money?"

Smedley slid his chair back, got up, and headed for the door. "No, I don't. If I hear anything, I'll let you know." He stopped and turned around. "Hey, Sport, when my trial comes up, wish me luck." And he was gone.

"Well, there you have it," Detective Phillips said, standing. "We're back to square one. We have no evidence yet to implicate Smedley in the robbery." Phillips checked his watch. "I have to get back to my office. Keep in touch."

Brian's eyes squinted as he exited the station into the bright, July sunshine. As he mounted his bike, he said, "You were too easy on him. Smedley hasn't changed. He's still money hungry. He's still trying to outsmart us. To him, it's all a twisted game."

"Speaking of games," Sammy said, "where were all those tricky psychological techniques you were going to use on Smedley?"

"Well, you saw what happened," Brian replied. "He knew I was ready to use my psychology stuff on him, so he got out of there fast."

Sammy rolled his eyes and picked up his bike. "I guess I won't see you until tomorrow morning."

Brian frowned. "No. We're visiting my Aunt Catherine in Lancaster today. It's a family thing. I have to go along."

The boys parted, promising to meet at the shop the next morning.

Sammy welcomed the one-mile ride back home. He wanted room and time to think. A dead end was the worst enemy of problem solving. Until new clues turned up, Sammy was facing the dreaded dead end.

To solve a puzzle, Sammy needed the right pieces to put together. Where were they? Yes, they had a description of the robbers from which the police artist made a sketch. They had the car used in the heist. They had hairs found in the car. What Sammy needed now were some straight pieces, the pieces that formed the framework of the puzzle. He certainly didn't get any from Lloyd Smedley.

Traveling east on Rt. 340 into Bird-in-Hand during tourist season was no easy task. Sammy's bike had competition with Amish scooters, horses and buggies, tourists' vehicles, and local cars and trucks.

Sammy rode his bike on the shoulder of the road, or as locals called it, the buggy lane. When traffic piled up behind the slow-moving buggies, the Amish pulled over and rode on the shoulder. After the faster moving traffic passed, the buggies reclaimed the road, only to repeat the maneuver seconds later.

The young detective shared the shoulder with the Amish—in buggies, on scooters, those pulling wagons, and those walking. It wasn't until he approached the concrete underpass that sidewalks appeared in front of houses. For safer traveling, Sammy switched over to the sidewalk that continued along under the concrete underpass.

Then it hit him, a straightedge to the back of his head. And not the puzzle straightedge he was thinking about earlier. This time it was a two-by-four.

CHAPTER SIX

S ammy had just come out from the underpass. The blow caused him to tumble from his bike and land face down on the sidewalk.

Two figures, both wearing ski masks, came up from behind. One grabbed Sammy and yanked him to his feet. Still groggy, Sammy jabbed his arm backward, plowing his elbow into somebody's mid-section. A moan erupted from the ski mask. Another blow from the piece of wood sent Sammy toward the sidewalk. On the way down, his head struck the concrete wall, and he lay still. On his back and stunned, he looked up through the haze.

Two hooded figures loomed above him. Their shapes told him that one was male, the other was female. "You stay away from Lloyd Smedley. You hear me? You stay away. He don't want to see you," the male thug said, kicking Sammy again and again.

"Hey, easy. That's enough," the hooded female said, pulling at her friend's arm. "Let's go. He's got the message."

By this time, some of the tourists and locals noticed that someone was in trouble. One car from Ohio pulled over to the side of the road, stopping traffic. A man and woman emerged and rushed toward the commotion. An Amish man and two boys, who were waiting for the bus to Lancaster, crossed the road to offer help. At the same time, the two hooded figures darted up the steps to the top of the concrete wall and vanished.

Sammy grimaced as he slowly raised himself up on one elbow. He waited a few seconds, then with the aid of the Amish man and the boys, stood, feeling the aches and pains. His body parts seemed to be working okay. Nothing was broken. Maybe a couple of ribs were bruised.

"I'm all right," he assured the people who had gathered. He picked up his bike, leaned on it, and hobbled home.

After he reassured his parents that time would cure his injuries, Sammy confined himself to bed. His mother applied ice packs to the lump on his head and bruised ribs and insisted he get a lot of rest.

Sleep was not what Sammy wanted. He wanted to focus on the common denominator in the case. The robbery: a male and a female. The attack: a male and a female. He sat up in bed. *What was the connection between the attackers and Lloyd Smedley?* he wondered. "Stay away from Lloyd Smedley," they had said. Smedley sounded sincere when he claimed he hadn't stolen the money. What did he have to gain by putting on his 'I-learned-my-lesson' act? Sammy's head was starting to spin. Perhaps Brian was right. Smedley was playing a game with him.

Chapter Seven

The next morning, it was business as usual at the Bird-in-Hand Country Store. Mrs. Wilson was in the quilt room, unfolding a wedding-ring pattern quilt for a customer's inspection. Mr. Wilson manned the cash register as he talked to several locals about the recent robbery. Sammy, still feeling the effects of the 'stay-away-from-Lloyd Smedley' threat, was with Brian at the baseball card counter. The topic of discussion was the attack on Sammy by the two hooded thugs. Visual signs of the attack were a lump on the head and bruises on his face.

"You took a kicking and kept right on ticking. Right, Sammy?" Brian said.

Before Sammy could react to his friend's intended humor, Detective Phillips and Mary Fisher entered the store. This was Mary's first time in the shop since the robbery. Everyone was anxious to express their sorrow regarding the terrible experience that she and Mrs. King endured. Mary Fisher immediately became the center of attention.

Detective Phillips whisked the boys into the back room for privacy. "I thought you should know what Mary told me at the station," Phillips whispered. "Her suspicion, by the way, confirms the lab's report on the hairs found in the car."

"What's that?" Sammy asked, anticipating some puzzle pieces.

"When things calmed down and Mary and Mrs. King went home to rest, they realized something. They both agreed that the robbers weren't as old as they first reported. They wore a lot of hair and make-up." Phillips smiled. "The lab report said the hairs came from cheap wigs."

Sammy moved and winced.

"What happened to you?" Phillips asked. "That's not dirt on your face, is it?"

Sammy told the details of the ambush by a hooded male and female. He finished by saying, "The two who attacked me were rather young, I believe."

Phillips entered the information into his notebook. "What are the chances that these two are the robbers?" he asked.

"A one hundred percent good chance," Brian said.

"Even so, we still don't know who they are," Sammy added.

"Have you been threatened by anyone lately?" Phillips asked, and then smiled. "Someone not wearing a ski mask."

"How about David Schultz and Angie Lowe?" Brian said.

"Well?" Phillips said, looking at Sammy.

"David wanted his money returned on a baseball card that he bought last week. He returned again today. I didn't refund the money because the card was bent after he bought it. He got mad and, well, you know what happens. He said things he didn't mean."

"Hey, look who's standing outside the shop," Brian announced, glancing past the people and out the front window.

Sammy and the detective moved to get a better view.

"It's David Schultz," Sammy said. "I wonder what he's doing?"

"So that's our David Schultz, is it?" Phillips said. "Wait here. I'll be back."

The boys followed Phillips into the next room. He excused himself past the women and joined David outside. Sammy watched and tried to imagine the conversation between the two. As they talked, David's expression changed from guilt to remorse. *Was David Schultz confessing to the crime?* Sammy wondered. *Will this be it? The case solved?* Sammy had mixed feelings. *The pieces of the puzzle can't come together like this*, he thought. *It's too simple, and David isn't that kind of guy, or is he?*

Interrogation time was over. Phillips marched David into the shop and motioned the boys to follow them into the back room.

"Sammy, David has something to say to you," the detective said.

David glanced down. "Paul bent the card, the boy that was with me on Saturday. Paul did it. He told me. It happened like you said. The card bent when he put it back into the holder."

For Brian, that didn't eliminate David from the brutal attack on Sammy the day before. Brian stood tall, squinted, and in his deepest voice asked, "Did you hit Sammy with the stick once or twice?"

David looked surprised. "What stick? What are you talking about?"

"Brian, don't go there," Sammy said.

"David was standing outside," Phillips said, "trying to get up the nerve to apologize to you."

"And the money," Brian said. "What about the robbery?"

"He claims he had nothing to do with it," Phillips said.

"That's right, and I'm sorry I gave you all that hassle, Sammy." David glanced up at the detective. "Can I go now?"

"Yeah, go ahead."

They watched as David left the shop.

"I don't know," Phillips said. "I have a feeling about that kid. He claims he has an alibi. He was with his girlfriend, Angie, at the Kitchen Kettle Village. If you can believe that. Anyway, I'll check it out."

Mrs. Wilson entered the room carrying a carton box. "Sammy, here's a FedEx package for you. Did you order something?"

"No," Sammy said, taking the package. He checked the shipping label. It was for him, alright.

Brian crowded the box and pointed at the return address. "It's from Nikon Electronics, New York."

Sammy hesitated and inspected the box, trying to guess its contents.

"Hey, it might be a bomb," Brian said.

"There's only one way to find out," Phillips said. "Open it."

Mrs. Wilson returned with a small knife. "Here, use this."

Brian backtracked quickly to the doorway as his friend sliced through the tape. Sammy carefully lifted the cardboard flaps. Underneath was the styrofoam packaging that protected the contents. When that was stripped away, a box depicting Nikon binoculars remained.

"Those are expensive," Phillips said, noting the model number. "They're better than the pair I use." He lifted his arm, checked the time, and bolted for the main room. "I have to take Mary home. I'll keep in touch."

"Okay," Sammy said in reply, slipping the optical instrument from its final wrapping.

No one gave Detective Phillips a respectable good-bye. The binoculars had become the center of attention when pulled from the box.

"Wow," Brian said. "If you didn't order these, then someone mailed you a great gift. Who sent it?"

Sammy checked the shipping label again. "It was sent to me at this address." He shrugged and rechecked the packaging. "The only other things in here are the packing slip and the paid receipt of the purchase."

Brian pulled Sammy's arm down and noted the final cost. "Wow, $1,218," he said.

The phone rang in the other room. "Sammy, it's for you," Mr. Wilson said.

Sammy took the binoculars with him and answered the phone. "Hello," he said.

"Did you receive the binoculars?" The voice was strained, as though the caller was trying to disguise it.

Sammy pressed the receiver to his ear. "Yes, I did. Who is this?"

"I'm the person who used a two-by-four to get your attention."

CHAPTER EIGHT

The muffled voice was recognizable as the male voice from the day before. "Hey, detective boy, I'm going to give you a chance to recover the old lady's money."

"Did you and your girlfriend steal it?" Sammy asked, hoping for a 'yes' answer.

"That's for me to know and you to find out. Listen. I'm only going to say this once. Go now, and take the binoculars with you. From Rt. 340, turn left onto North Weavertown Road. Go about one mile to Number 1090 on your right. Focus the binoculars on the Amish farm. You'll see something out of place."

"And when I find it?" Sammy asked.

"It's a clue, detective boy. It's a clue."

Click.

"Hello, hello," Sammy said to a dead connection and then hung up.

"Is something wrong?" Mrs. Wilson asked, carrying the packaging material to the trash container under the counter.

Sammy reached into the box that had contained the binoculars and retrieved the neck strap and operating instructions. He clicked the strap to the binoculars and centered it around his neck. He crammed the instructions into his pants pocket. "Come on, Brian. We're going bird watching."

CHAPTER NINE

The bikes, wheeled in off the macadam road, met the resistance of the newly-plowed field. Amish privacy could not be invaded by riding up the farm lane to get a closer look. The boys had to be satisfied with viewing the farm from afar, thus the reason for the binoculars.

"This is good enough," Sammy said. "Stop here." He let his bike rest on its side atop the soft soil.

Brian did the same and then squinted at the old farm. "We're to look at the farm for a clue to the robbery, using a $1,200 pair of binoculars supplied by the robbers." Brian shook his head. "I don't get it."

"Maybe he's one of those guys who wants to get caught. Let's not look a gift horse in the mouth," Sammy said. "Clues are hard to come by. I say we take what we can get."

The farm was at least 200 yards away. Green corn stalks waved beyond the plowed field, underlining several barns, silos, and the farmhouse. Sammy counted four trees. Nothing unusual presented itself.

Sammy raised the binoculars to his face. The image was blurred. He made some adjustments and tried again. He saw a windmill behind the house. A clothesline held three dresses, four black trousers, and three bedsheets. A birdhouse topped a pole near the farmhouse. A vegetable garden showed signs of green and red tomatoes.

Sammy moved the binoculars to his left. A large, compressed air holding tank sat on the roof of a small shed nestled against the main barn. The shed housed the gasoline-run compressor engine. The super sleuth saw compressed air hoses running from the tank, across the barn siding, and disappearing inside.

"Do you see it? Do you see the clue?" Brian asked.

"The voice said that we would see something out of place," Sammy said, slowly moving the binoculars around. "It looks like a typical Amish farm—no electric wires, no car or tractor, and no TV antennas."

Sammy stripped the binoculars from around his neck and handed them to Brian. "Here, you look. See if you can see anything unusual. You might have to adjust them to your eyes."

Brian put the strap around his neck and looked. "Boy, you have to hold them still or the image dances all over the place. Hey, there's a schoolhouse up the hill beyond the house."

"Concentrate on the farm," Sammy said, anxious to reclaim the binoculars. "We're looking for anything out of place."

"I know. I know," Brian said. "Oh, I can see a birdhouse on a pole."

"Brian, a birdhouse is not out of place on an Amish farm. Try looking for something you don't see."

Brian lowered the binoculars and looked for a smile from Sammy. He didn't see one. "You're kidding. Right, Sammy?"

Sammy shook his head. "I didn't see an outhouse," Sammy said. "However, that can't be the clue, because most farmhouses have indoor plumbing."

Brian handed the binoculars to Sammy. "Here, you look for something that isn't there. You're better at it than I am."

The amateur detectives spent an hour more searching for anything that might pass for a clue. After Brian took the binoculars for the fifth time, Sammy felt like a floundering fish, definitely a fish out of water. Spending time looking for 'who knows what' was ridiculous. Not only would he have to discover something as a clue, he had to decipher what it meant.

Sammy had solved enough puzzles to know something was wrong. The equation was lopsided. A $1,200 pair of binoculars was on one side of the scale, and a phantom clue was on the other side. Sammy knew Lloyd Smedley from the previous investigation. He had no money. If Smedley stole the money, would he have spent it on expensive binoculars to find a clue to nail him as the thief? Definitely not.

"Come on, Brian," Sammy said. "Let's pack up and go home. This is silly. It's better we use the binoculars to spy on Mrs. Thomas' son."

"Yeah, I was thinking the same thing," Brian said, feeling the effects of the sun on his face and arms and pressure on his bladder. "I have to go to the bathroom."

When the boys' bikes were back on the road, Sammy said, "Let's use the restroom at the Bird-in-Hand Family Restaurant, and then maybe get some information about William Thomas from his coworkers. We'll meet in my bedroom at nine sharp tomorrow morning."

"I have a dentist appointment at nine," Brian said. "It will have to be later."

"Okay," Sammy said, "come whenever you're finished. I'll have a plan of action drawn up by then. We'll track down William's money source."

"You know what I was thinking, Sammy?"

"It's hard to know sometimes, Brian."

"What if William's money source was the buggy heist?"

Chapter Ten

B rian ran up the stairs and into Sammy's bedroom at 10:30 the next morning. He collapsed
back on the bed, his chest moving rapidly.

"Calm down, Brian. There's no hurry."

"Why is Detective Phillips downstairs in the
shop, talking to your parents?"

"I didn't know he was there," Sammy said.
"Maybe he has more information about the robbery."

Heavy thumping was heard coming up the steps.

"Hey, Sammy, you in there?" Detective Phillips
said as he peeped into the bedroom.

Sammy stood. "Yeah, come in."

"Your father said it would be alright to come up,"
Phillips said. His impressive figure added distinction
to the room. Glancing at the assortment of books and
apparatus before him, he stated, "You have a well-
equipped room here."

The detective's eyes continued to survey the
walls, the floor, and the binoculars on Sammy's desk.
His search ended at the bed.

Sammy detected a look of concern on Phillips' face. "Something wrong?" he asked.

For the first time since entering the bedroom, Phillips' dark eyes fixed on Sammy. "Do you mind if I look under your bed?"

Brian giggled and hopped off the bed. "What are you looking for, a dead body?"

Detective Phillips didn't answer. He got down on his hands and knees and glanced under the bed. To get a better look, he slid two piles of magazines to one side. He grabbed at something and stood. In the detective's right hand was a large bundle of money, secured with a rubber band.

With a dour expression, Phillips asked, "Is this money yours?"

Chapter Eleven

"I hate to put you through this, Sammy. This is a nightmare for me. Were you boys involved in the robbery of Amos King's money?"

Sammy and Brian were stunned. They couldn't believe what they were seeing and hearing. This was the first time they were the subjects of a criminal interrogation.

"No, we were not involved in the robbery," Sammy said, "and I don't know anything about the money you found under my bed. I'm as surprised as you are."

The detective dropped the money into an evidence bag. "Do you know anything about another bundle like this one that we found in a plastic bag buried in a field off North Weavertown Road?"

"No, I don't," Sammy said.

Detective Phillips pressed on. "When I have the bundles dusted for prints, yours won't be on them. Is that what you are saying?"

Sammy nodded and said, "That's what I'm saying."

Phillips ran his hand over his face and shook his head. "Sammy, Detective Wetzel matched your bike wheel treads to those we found this morning near the buried money. I bet your sneaker prints will match, too."

"I got a match," came a voice from below the stairway.

"That was Detective Wetzel," Phillips said. "He just inspected your bike, Brian, and you heard what he said. Your bike was there, too. Boys come clean. Where's the rest of the money?"

Brian wished he was still in the dentist's office.

Sammy picked up the binoculars. "Of course, we were there in the field off North Weavertown Road. Somebody told us to use these binoculars to look at the farm for a clue." Even as he said it, it felt like a lame excuse.

Phillips appeared skeptical. "Where did you get the money to buy the pair of binoculars? They are expensive."

Redness appeared on Sammy's face. His voice rose with a hardness to it. "You were there when the package arrived. You know I didn't order the binoculars."

"Yes, and you didn't expect me to be there, so you acted surprised and claimed you knew nothing about them. Yet they came addressed to you directly from the dealer in New York. You had to prepay for the binoculars to be shipped to you."

Blood veins were evident on Sammy's forehead. "Can't you see that we're being set up? The two thieves want you to believe we stole the money."

"Now, why would they do that? They have the money. Why get you involved?"

"It's Smedley. He wants to punish us for his arrest," Brian said.

"Wait a minute," Sammy said. "Who told you to look under my bed and in the field for the money?"

"I got a phone call. He didn't identify himself. He said he overheard you and Brian talking about sticking money under your bed. He followed you to the farm and saw you bury the money."

Sammy saw a glimmer of light. "You have caller ID on your phone. Did you trace the number?"

"Yes. It was from a pay phone. Someone didn't want to get involved. He probably is a friend of yours." Phillips reached for his handcuffs, and then stopped. He couldn't believe what he was about to do. But if he didn't arrest Sammy and Brian, he would be accused of favoritism. "You're both under arrest for theft," he said finally.

"Wait," Sammy said. "We can prove we didn't steal the money. We have an alibi for the time of the robbery." He paused to get his facts straight. "The robbery happened a little after 9 o'clock Monday morning. Right?"

"That's right," Phillips said, wishing Sammy could resolve the conflict.

"At that time, Brian and I were visiting and talking to a Mrs. Betty Thomas on Ronks Road. Her husband's name is Frank. She wants us to discover the source of her son's recently-acquired money." Sammy took a deep breath and relaxed somewhat. "Whoever wants to frame us didn't count on us having an alibi for the time of the robbery."

The detective turned and faced Brian, who was nodding his head frantically. "We can settle this right now," he said. "Let me give Mrs. Betty Thomas a call. Is she a friend of yours by any chance?"

Brian's head shifted gears and was now shaking no. "She doesn't even resemble any of my friends," he said. "We just met her Monday morning."

Phillips went downstairs, gave the evidence bag of money to Detective Wetzel, and used the Wilson's phone to check the boys' alibi. When he returned to the bedroom, his face was grim. "Sorry, boys. It was a nice try, but Mrs. Thomas never heard of you."

CHAPTER TWELVE

Sammy and Brian couldn't believe it. What was happening? The walls of truth, honesty, and respect were tumbling down around the young, aspiring detectives. Their apparent reality was full of holes and not holding water.

Detective Phillips was perplexed, but the evidence against the boys pointed to their guilt. Because of Sammy and Brian's reputation and their invaluable help on the previous case, Phillips thought he owed the boys a reprieve. If it was a conspiracy against the boys, it was an elaborate one. Maybe the woman he spoke to on the phone was the wrong Mrs. Thomas. To make sure, he took the boys to confront Mrs. Betty Thomas on Ronks Road.

"That's the house," Brian said from the back seat, "the one on the corner."

"I'll do the talking," the detective said as they approached the front door. "You boys just show your pretty faces."

A woman in her thirties opened the door on the first knock. "Yes?" she said.

"Hi, I'm Detective Phillips. I believe I talked to you earlier over the phone. Are you Betty Thomas?"

"Yes."

"And you have a husband, Frank?"

"I told you all this before. Are these the boys?"

"Did you see and talk to them Monday morning?"

"I wasn't here Monday morning. I was shopping."

"Are you sure you weren't here Monday morning, talking to these boys?"

"I'm sure. I go shopping every Monday."

"Does anyone else live here with you besides your husband?"

"No."

"You have no son?"

"That's right."

"Was your husband here Monday morning?"

"No, he was at work."

Sammy raised his hand.

Phillips nodded.

"May I talk now?" Sammy asked.

"Go ahead."

"This is not the Mrs. Thomas we talked to. She was older, heavier, and wore a large floppy hat and sunglasses. She took us to the back porch to talk about her son."

Mrs. Thomas frowned. "I have no children," she said.

Desperate to gain points for their side, Sammy said, "Mrs. Thomas, we haven't seen the back of your house. We just got here. Do you have wicker furniture on your back porch?"

"Yes, I do."

"One sofa and two chairs."

"That's right."

"And you have several flower gardens in your backyard."

"Why, yes."

"And you have beige curtains at your kitchen window."

"That's right."

"See, we were here," Sammy added.

Detective Phillips shook his head. "It might prove you were here, but not necessarily Monday morning. I have no other choice. I have to arrest you and Brian."

Sammy showed no reason to smile, but he did. He could now appreciate the full extent of the sophisticated scheme that was designed to frame them. It was no use to fight the arrest. They would be taken to the police station, be booked, and then released on their own recognition. Sammy felt a concern for Brian's parents and his own. Only one option remained for Brian and himself; they had to uncover the real thieves.

CHAPTER THIRTEEN

The next morning, after the hullabaloo surrounding their arrest had lessened, Sammy and Brian did a little brainstorming. They were fighting for their reputations against a very clever villain.

"Let's assume the two who attacked me are the same two who took the money," Sammy said, sitting at his desk. "Does that tie Lloyd Smedley to the robbery?"

Brian sat on the bed. He was too tense to lie back and face the ceiling. "They warned you to stay away from Smedley. I'd say that makes Smedley the ringleader."

"What if the two who attacked me were not the robbers?" Sammy asked. "Then we could be dealing with two sets of young people, plus an older woman."

"You mean the fake Mrs. Thomas," Brian said to verify Sammy's comment.

"Let's start with the basics," Sammy said. "We have a teenage boy and girl who took the money. The older woman is with them in their attempt to frame us. Maybe she's the brains behind everything."

Brian wasn't buying it. "If this is just a plain robbery, why set up the plan to frame us? Why not take the money and run?"

"That's a good point, Brian," Sammy said, wanting to encourage his friend. "The person behind this must really hate us for some reason."

"So, where do we start?" Brian asked.

Sammy stood and headed for the door. "For starters, we can find out who ordered the binoculars. I'm going to call the dealer in New York right now. The phone number is on the packing slip."

While Sammy was phoning, Brian thought about the fake Mrs. Thomas. *She could be somebody's grandmother, or mother, or wife, or aunt, or neighbor, or . . . anyone.* He grimaced. *Will the police pursue other suspects now that they think that we are the robbers? What other suspects? There are none now that they accused Sammy and me. How could a sweet old lady take advantage of us? She even gave us lemonade.*

Sammy tramped into the bedroom and slammed the paper down on his desk. "Just once, I wish something would go our way. This case is giving me a headache." He plopped into his chair and closed his eyes.

Brian had never seen his friend behave like this before. Sammy always seemed to be in control of his emotions. Was he losing it? Brian wanted to hide. He couldn't stand seeing people in pain. "What happened?" he asked.

Sammy kept his eyes closed. "The pair of binoculars was paid with two $500 money orders and a $218 money order. The only name on it was the Turkey Hill Market in Smoketown that issued it."

Brian stood and jumped over to the desk. He produced his widest smile ever. "That's great! Turkey Hill can tell us who bought the money orders."

"Brian, don't be dumb. These people are smart. Do you think they'll let themselves be identified by marching into a Turkey Hill and buying $1,218 worth of money orders? If we go there now, they'll probably tell us that the person was dressed funny, wore a hooded sweatshirt, wore sunglasses, and had a hairy face."

Brian backed up to the bed. "Yeah, that was dumb of me."

"Brian, I'm sorry. I didn't mean it. I shouldn't assume anything. Look, go prove me wrong. Ride over to Turkey Hill and check on it. Tell them the money orders were bought Monday afternoon."

"That's right after the robbery," Brian said.

Sammy nodded. "They had the weekend before the robbery to put their scheme together. After the robbery, they were set to go. They planted the money here in the bedroom. Then they bought the money orders and ordered the binoculars in my name, giving my address. They followed us to the farm. After we left, they buried the money near our tire tracks and shoe prints, erasing their own shoe prints from the soil."

"The fake Mrs. Thomas and her non-existent son were part of the plan. Maybe she's the ringleader.

I was thinking how sweet she was to us, giving us lemonade."

"Well, that cunning woman handled her part well. She knew the routine of the Thomases. While the real Mrs. Thomas and her husband were away, she used the outside of the house. Remember how she had us take our bikes to the rear. Then she invited us up on the back porch where we couldn't be seen. Boy, was she clever. She offered us lemonade to keep us there while the robbery was taking place."

"She couldn't go into the locked house to get the lemonade, so she had it ready in a vacuum bottle on the porch."

Sammy collapsed into his chair and allowed his right hand to swing down and open a desk drawer. Sales slips from the shop went from one pile to another on the desk as he calculated the total. "My figures show I have $63 due me from the sale of baseball cards."

This annoyed Brian. "Shouldn't we be thinking of how we're going to become un-arrested?"

"First we list the names of those who hold a grudge against us. Second, we determine who had the means to frame us. Then, we have to prove it. That calls for us to become more clever than they are," Sammy said. "And I can think better and be more clever with money in my pocket."

Brian crossed his arms over his chest and grinned. "Yeah, and we'll have spending money in jail."

Sammy rose from his desk, clutching the sales receipts. "You get your own money, jail person."

"I hope they put us in the same cell," Brian said. "I hate suffering alone."

Sammy rolled his eyes, opened the bedroom door, and called down the stairs. "Dad, I figure I sold $63 worth of baseball cards. Is it okay if I take the money from the bank bag?"

"Sure, it's in the end table drawer."

Sammy knelt down and took the bag from the drawer. The green vinyl bag contained the money earned in the shop since Monday. They made deposits every Saturday. He unzipped the bag and selected three twenties and three one-dollar bills.

As Sammy returned the bag to the drawer, he smelled something strange. A foul odor. He waved the bills under his nose. The scent was familiar. Oil. It was the smell of oil. The amateur detective experienced an 'I've-been-here-before' feeling. *What was it about the oil smell?* he wondered. He examined the bills in his hand. The three twenty-dollar bills had a notch bent into the middle of each side. Yes, yes, yes. The last time Sammy smelled oil was at Steve Zook's woodshop when they opened Amos King's large wrench box. Certain facts had not been released to the media, but under the top tray containing wrenches, they found bundles of money held together with rubber bands.

Quickly, Sammy again opened the bank bag and inspected the other bills. Only one other twenty had a notch in the middle of each side. It, too, had an oily smell.

"Dad, Brian, look!" shouted Sammy. "We might have some of the robbery money here!"

Mr. Wilson bolted up the steps. He and Brian joined Sammy in the living room, where Sammy had them smell the money. He showed them the notches that could have been produced by rubber bands.

Brian looked at Sammy. "Not only is there money in oil, there's also oil in money. Hey, that's why money slips through my fingers so easily." Brian smiled, but discovered that his friend was not in the mood for his corny humor.

"Dad, do you remember who gave you these twenty-dollar bills?" Sammy asked.

"Not a chance," Mr. Wilson said. "You saw all the bills in the bag. There's no way I can remember who gave me those particular twenties over the last several days."

There has to be a way, Sammy thought. He pictured customers paying for their purchases. Most large sales were for quilts, costing hundreds of dollars. Sammy narrowed it down. "Okay, Dad, how about this? Four notched twenty-dollar bills were together. Can you recall any customer who made a purchase of around eighty dollars?"

Mr. Wilson sat in his overstuffed chair. "One customer bought old jewelry for seventy-five dollars. No, wait. She used a credit card."

Brian jumped back as the chair noisily expanded into a recliner. "Do what I do," Brian said. "Look at the ceiling and concentrate."

Sammy's father took a deep breath and closed his eyes. "Your friend who buys antiques bought the old table phonograph for one hundred dollars."

"George Burk," Sammy said. "He's not my friend. I just know him from coming into the shop and seeing him at auctions around the area. Did he pay cash for the phonograph?"

"Yes, he did. I remember because he asked the girl with him for extra money. He paid in twenties, as I recall."

Brian punched the air with his finger. "Ah, a young male and a young female."

While Sammy continued to encourage his father to recall and reveal details of other purchase transactions, Brian slipped into the bedroom. He returned, carrying Sammy's desk chair. He quietly placed the chair next to the recliner and motioned Sammy to sit. Brian stood back and grinned. This completed the picture. Sammy, the psychiatrist, was helping Mr. Wilson, his patient, probe for memories.

"Alright, anyone else?" Sammy urged.

"Do you remember Monday, after we heard about the robbery, and you and Brian left for the parking lot? Well, those musicians bought five Amish hats. Their total must have been $75 plus tax, because the hats sell for $15 each."

"Great," Sammy said. "There's at least another young male and young female. I bet Jenny Herr is Travis Wells' girlfriend. Which means she might do anything for him to help finance his band."

Brian's eyes squinted and darted toward Sammy. "And George Burk's girlfriend would do anything for him to start his antique shop. Right, Sammy?"

The super sleuth gave his partner a slight nod but continued with his father. "Anyone else, Dad?"

"We can eliminate most tourists, because they usually pay with traveler's checks, personal checks, or charge cards. A girl came in with her mother, local people. I know because I saw her before. She was the girl that was with David Schultz when he was arguing with you on Monday. I knew I had seen her before that."

"Angie Lowe," Sammy said.

"Yeah, she bought something for her mother," Mr. Wilson said.

"What was it?"

"Your mother waited on them, and I rang up the sale. She paid cash. Angie was holding the money. I know because her mother didn't want her to spend so much money on her."

Sammy leaned forward in his chair. "Try to visualize what they carried out the door. Reliving the event sometimes jogs the memory."

Mr. Wilson closed his eyes and remained still for ten seconds. "It was a small wall hanging. Yep, that's what it was. Her mother wanted to carry it, but Angie said no, because her mother's birthday wasn't until Friday. They were laughing and arguing at the same time."

"And she could have paid with these twenty-dollar bills," Sammy said.

Mr. Wilson flipped the recliner upright and stood. "The smaller wall hangings are ninety dollars, so it's possible, yes. I have to get back downstairs with your mother. If I think of any more, I'll let you know."

The boys returned to the bedroom. Brian replaced the chair behind the desk. The four twenties were placed on display, side by side, on the desk. Sammy slid into his chair and gazed thoughtfully at the creased bills. Brian perched on the edge of the bed and gazed at Sammy. He knew not to interfere with Sammy's thought processes. With new evidence at hand, the master was at work.

"Brian, we now have three sets of suspects—Travis Wells and Jenny Herr, David Schultz and Angie Lowe, and George Burk and his girlfriend. If these twenties are part of the stolen money, then the guilty ones are one of these pairs. Any one of them could have snuck up the stairs and planted the money under my bed. More suspects might be out there, but these are our suspects so far."

"Don't forget Smedley and the fake Mrs. Thomas."

"They are on my list. We must get evidence by connecting any of them to the stolen car, the attack on me, or to the stolen money. Now, about the stolen car. Since the ignition wires were not tampered with, then there must be another key besides the extra one Glen Clover has in his house."

"Where would the third key come from?"

"If Glen loaned his car to someone, that person could have a key made before he returned the car."

"Right," Brian said. "I bet one of our suspects borrowed Glen's car at one time. Let's go ask him."

"Another solution exists, Brian. What if Glen Clover's car wasn't stolen?"

Brian's mouth dropped open. "You mean Glen Clover used his car in the robbery, abandoned it in the Farmer's Market parking lot, and then reported it stolen?"

"It's possible."

"But he said he was in bed until 9:00 Monday morning," Brian said.

Sammy raised his eyebrows and shrugged. "How do we know that?"

"That's easy," Brian said. "We can go and ask his mother."

"Yes, we could ask Mrs. Clover, but the more I think about it, the more I wonder."

"What?" Brian asked.

Sammy took a deep breath. "I wonder if Mrs. Clover makes good lemonade?"

CHAPTER FOURTEEN

Glen Clover was visible to the teenage detectives. The garage doors were open all the way, and he was inside, working a paintbrush. His blue car sat in the driveway.

"The garage doesn't look like a health hazard this time," Brian said to Sammy, recalling the dust storm on their last visit.

Sammy stood astride his bike. "He's painting. He doesn't want sawdust flying around."

Glen saw the boys. "Hey, Sammy, Brian, park your bikes next to the car. Don't get too close in here. I'm painting." Glen made his last pass with the wet brush and then scraped the excess paint back into the can. "Wait until I clean myself up, and I'll be back."

The boys watched as Glen vanished into the house, taking the paintbrush with him. Ten seconds later, Mrs. Clover appeared at the second-floor window. She smiled and waved.

Sammy and Brian returned the courtesy but wondered what was going on behind the pleasant face. *What would she look like wearing a large floppy hat over a red wig, sunglasses, and cotton in her mouth to puff out her cheeks?*

"What's up?" Glen asked, as the screen door slammed shut behind him.

"I see that the police returned your car," Sammy said. "Is it working okay?"

"Yeah, great," Glen said. "What do you want?"

"From the time your father gave you the car, how many people have you allowed to use it?"

"Why?"

"It's possible one of them had a duplicate key made."

The blank stare told Sammy that the idea never occurred to Glen. His eyes went up and to his right. "My cousin used it once to bring her mother home from the hospital."

"What's her name?"

"Angie Lowe."

"Angie Lowe is your cousin?" Brian asked.

"Yeah, why?"

Brian glanced at Sammy, then back at Glen, and shrugged. "No reason. I know her, that's all. Isn't she David Schultz's girlfriend?"

"The baseball card nut? Yeah, at the moment," Glen said.

"Did anybody else use your car?"

Glen shook his head. "No, she's the only one." He leaned back against his car, shook his head, and smiled. "Don't even think it. I grew up with Angie. She's shy and timid. No way would she commit a robbery."

"Do you have a picture of Angie that I could borrow?" Sammy asked.

Glen nodded. "In the family album. Wait, I'll be right back."

Glen returned in five minutes with a photo of his cousin. "Here, but return it soon. I have to put it back."

"Thanks, I will," Sammy said, looking at the photo. It was a headshot of the blond girl. He slipped it into the backpack attached to his bike. "Where does Angie live?"

"Her family just moved. I believe over on Horseshoe Road somewhere."

"Do you have a girlfriend, Glen?" Sammy asked.

Before Glen could answer, the screen door opened and slammed shut. "You boys look serious out here. What's going on?" Mrs. Clover asked.

"Mrs. Clover, can I speak to you alone?" Sammy asked.

Sammy walked down the driveway, and Mrs. Clover followed. Brian remained with Glen.

"Because Glen's car was used in the robbery, we're trying to eliminate him as a suspect. He told us that, at the time of the robbery, he was with you in the backyard planting some bushes. Is that true?"

She looked at Sammy and smiled. "You're a sly one, Sammy. You know that's not true. He told you he got out of bed at 9:00, had breakfast, and went to the garage. That's exactly what he did."

"I had to ask. You understand, don't you?" Sammy said sheepishly.

Mrs. Clover shrugged and glanced back at her son. "I already went through this with the cops."

"Thanks for the information," Sammy said and headed for his bike. "Let's go, Brian."

Brian pointed inside the garage. "Hey, Sammy, see the painted box in there and the painted lid beside it? After the paint dries, Glen is going to put hinges on it."

"It will be my treasure box for things too good to throw away," Glen said.

Like Amos King's money, Sammy thought to himself as he pedaled away.

Brian soon caught up. "Does Mrs. Clover fit the part of Mrs. Thomas?"

"Maybe with a red wig, some padding under her clothes, and a little cotton stuffed in her cheeks."

Brian nodded. "I was thinking the same thing."

"Here's something else you were probably thinking," Sammy said sarcastically. "Angie Lowe has a connection to the car and also had access to the stairs leading to my bedroom. That leads to a bigger question. Could the young male and female robbers be Angie Lowe and Glen Clover, her cousin, or Angie Lowe and David Schultz, her boyfriend?"

"That's easy to find out. Let's go and ask her."

"Easy?"

"Sure. I'll use your bind technique on her. I'll say, 'Did you and Glen Clover steal the money, or was it you and David Schultz?'"

Sammy rolled his eyes. "We'll go see Angie Lowe, but let me do the talking."

CHAPTER FIFTEEN

The way to Angie Lowe was through David Schultz. David's address was well known to Sammy. At one time, baseball card swapping occurred weekly at David's house. Now, every transaction was cash. David Schultz wanted it that way.

As the boys neared the house, a FedEx truck pulled away. They saw David with a thin package tucked under his arm. His back was to them as he headed for his car.

"Hey, David!" Sammy yelled. "May we talk to you a minute?"

Recognizing the voice, David hesitated and then threw the package into the car through the open window. He whirled around and threw his hands upward. "It's okay. It was my fault. I'm sorry. What more can I say?"

The boys rode to within ten feet of him and straddled their bikes.

"No, no, it's not about the card," Sammy said. "I wanted to ask you about Angie."

"What about her?"

"Can you tell me where she lives?"

"Yeah, 445 Horseshoe Road. Why?"

Sammy wasn't sure how to proceed, so he took a chance. "Some time ago, Angie borrowed her cousin's car to take her mother home from the hospital. I believe she had a key made for the car. Do you know where she had it made?"

David opened the car door, proposing a short conversation. "No, you'll have to ask her, but there's a key maker over in the Mill Creek flea market near Smoketown. That's where I'd go."

"Okay, thanks," Sammy said. He nodded toward the car seat. "Are you still buying rookie cards?"

"No, these aren't rookies. They're just a couple of Ted Williams cards," David said and slammed the door. The car peeled away from the curb, heading in the direction of Horseshoe Road.

"Now where do we go?" Brian asked.

Sammy checked his watch. "We still have time. Maybe the key maker at Mill Creek Market can identify Angie as a former car key buyer."

Brian grinned. "That's why you got her picture from Glen."

"And there's something else," Sammy said. "She passed the Mill Creek Market on the way to the hospital."

"Yeah, but first she stopped and had a copy made of the car key. Right, Sammy?"

Sammy frowned. "I hope the answer to our problem is that simple, Brian."

Brian stood tall and puffed out his chest. "Hey, simple is my middle name."

Sammy nodded and sat up on his bike. "Brian, every time I think of simple, I think of you."

CHAPTER SIXTEEN

The sign outside advertised antiques, flowers, crafts, and seasonal items. Buses were welcomed. The open-air Mill Creek Market sat back 50 feet from the old Philadelphia Pike. Metal frameworks supported two white corrugated roofs, creating two open-air rectangular shelters. Tables and counters displayed an array of merchandise. On the outside, scattered around, were flowers, metal stars, and antique pieces.

Sammy and Brian were pleased when, halfway through the first shelter, they saw a large wooden key, dangling from an overhead pipe. On the table beneath were baseball cards, miniature cars, and a rack of blank keys. A middle-aged man was bent over, brushing away metal filings from the key-cutting machine.

"Pardon me, sir," Sammy said to get the man's attention.

The vendor looked up and was as stunned as Sammy and Brian. "No, pardon me," Lloyd Smedley finally said. Then with a sneer, he added, "That's a joke, Sport."

Brian instinctively moved behind Sammy. Smedley had held a knife on Brian in their previous caper. Dreams kept the incident alive for Brian. Detective Phillips couldn't protect them here as he had when they questioned Smedley at the police station. Brian glanced around and found some comfort being in a crowded market.

"Don't you know that I'm not a suspect anymore?" Smedley asked. "The police caught the real thieves. I believe it was two boys by the name of Sammy Wilson and Brian Helm. Yep, they were caught with the stolen money."

Sammy leaned closer to Smedley. "We were framed, and you know it."

"Hey, Sport, we'll be in jail together." Smedley smiled. "Oh, I forgot. You said you were framed. I can't say the same for myself since you caught me red-handed." Smedley tilted his head sideways to get a glimpse of Brian. "I was hoping you were guilty. I so wanted to visualize Brian dressed as a girl."

Sammy pointed to the key cutting machine. "It would be easy for you to make a key to fit Glen Clover's car."

"Only if I had the original key."

Sammy held up the photo of Angie Lowe. "Did you ever copy a car key for this girl?"

Smedley shook his head. "Nope, never done it."

"Did you ever make a copy of Glen Clover's car key for anyone?"

"How would I know if a certain key is for a certain car?" Smedley shrugged. "People bring in keys. I copy them. I don't ask what they belong to."

"Do you know of any other key makers in this area?" Sammy asked.

Smedley sat on a stool that was next to him. "No, not around here. The closest would be the Wizard Lock in Lancaster."

Sammy noticed some items stapled to a wooden support pole next to the counter. One was an old dollar bill in a plastic sleeve. The other two were faded photographs.

Smedley saw Sammy leaning toward the pole. "It's the first dollar I took in here at the market six years ago. This here is a picture of my family, and this photo is me, standing behind this same counter six years ago."

"You had a mustache and a beard then."

"I might try it again. Hey, when you two are in prison and you see a gray-bearded man, that might be me."

Sammy raised his eyebrows and turned. "Thanks for the warning," he said and pushed Brian ahead of him.

Smedley's laughing voice trailed them as they walked away. "Hey, Sport, when you're ready, come back, and I'll make you a key to fit your jail cell. I already have mine."

"Walk faster," Brian said. "People are looking at us."

"Get used to it, Brian," Sammy said. "People will continue to stare until we clear ourselves."

Brian nudged Sammy's arm and pointed. "Hey, look who's out there."

George Burk was placing some antique pieces on the ground. One was an old wooden sled; the other was a rusted milk can.

"Oh, good," Sammy said and hurried in that direction.

The haphazard placement of items on the ground created a navigation challenge for Brian. A challenge he lost in his attempt to follow his friend. He tripped over an old rusted hand plow, stumbled among wire egg baskets, and ended up on his knees, hugging a large potted flower.

Sammy glanced back and shook his head. "Brian, I know you love flowers, but now is not the time."

"Okay, okay," Brian said as he lurched back on his knees and tried to reshape the egg baskets.

"Hi, George," Sammy said when George glanced his way. "Are you buying or selling?"

George snapped his shoulders back and adjusted his baseball cap. "I'm selling. You know how it is, buy low and sell high."

"I'm sure you heard of our situation regarding the robbery," Sammy said

George wiped his hands down over his jeans. "Yeah, for what it's worth, I don't believe you and Brian did it. You said you were framed, and that's the way it is."

"Someone planted some of the stolen money in my bedroom on Monday. You were there, George. In fact, you were upstairs using the bathroom. You could have entered my bedroom and hid the money."

Sammy watched George for signs of guilt—the downcast eyes, the moving Adam's apple. George was a wheeler-dealer, a shrewd, young man. Lies were a way of life. Any evidence of guilt was tainted by years of experience.

"Sure, I could have planted the money," George said. "And so could all the others who were in your store that day. If you want a suspect, I'll give you one. You know the girl that's in that local rock band? They were in the store when I was there. I saw her sneak up the steps."

"Jenny Herr," Brian said.

"Yeah, that's the one," George said.

Sammy remembered Jenny Herr and the drummer going to look at the Amish hats while Travis Wells talked to him. *Was that the way they planned it?* Sammy wondered. *Travis kept me busy while Jenny hid the evidence.*

"People go up those steps thinking it's part of the store," Brian said. "Your parents should have a sign there, saying it's a private residence above."

George added, "Or put on a door and keep it locked."

A motor roared in the parking lot. In seconds, a truck appeared from nowhere, its wheels spitting stones. Before the boys could react, the truck skidded to a halt, barely missing a deformed egg basket.

A girl's head sprouted from the window. "Well, are you coming or not? It always takes you an hour to do five minutes of work. Come on. I have to get home and cleaned up."

The eighteen-year-old girl was no beauty. Her dark hair was matted, and her face was covered with meanness. Her tirade was aimed at George Burk.

"I'm coming! I'm coming!" George shouted back. "That's my sister Amy. She has no patience," he said softly to Sammy and Brian, and then ran around the front of the truck and climbed inside.

The girl gave a departing sneer to Sammy and Brian and headed the truck for the exit.

"Are you thinking what I'm thinking, Brian?"

Brian saw his friend still staring at the truck. "You mean that George and his sister could be the robbers?"

Sammy nodded. "Amy looks like a mean one."

"Sisters are like that," Brian said. "I have one, and that's enough. Do you know what I always wondered, Sammy?"

Sammy shook his head. "Brian, you constantly keep me guessing."

Brian leaned over and touched a flower. "Why are people nicer to strangers than they are to their own family members?"

"That's a profound question, Brian. You surprise me sometimes."

Brian's face brightened. "I'm full of profound stuff. The more I wonder, the profounder I get."

Sammy checked his watch. "Right now, you better get yourself home to eat. I'll do the same. Do you have anything going on family-wise this evening?"

"No, why?"

"Travis Wells' band is playing at the Ephrata Fair." Sammy smiled. "I'm anxious to hear his Amish music creation."

"Yeah, I bet you are," Brian said. "My profound wondering tells me you want to interrogate Jenny Herr. Right, Sammy?"

"Brian, your profounder just found me out."

CHAPTER SEVENTEEN

B oth sides of the main street were lined with food stands, games of chance, and rides. A sizeable stage was constructed four feet off the ground for entertainment. Young and old filled the streets, forming currents and swirls as they sampled the fare.

Sammy and Brian approached the stage as Travis Wells and his group were connecting and adjusting their electronic equipment. It appeared to be Amish at work. The young men wore black hats. Suspenders stretched over lavender shirts and buttoned to black trousers. The lone girl, Jenny Herr, wore a black bonnet and an apron over a lavender dress. Amish clothes made color coordination easy.

Before Sammy and Brian said anything, Travis Wells looked down and said, "We don't converse with criminals."

The statement caught the boys off guard. Since their arrest, they had received many odd stares and mixed comments; they still couldn't shake the fabricated shame forced upon them.

Travis' stern face broke into a grin. "Hey, I'm kidding. If you say you were framed, you were framed. Are you here to bid us good luck?"

"We're here to see Jenny," Sammy said.

Travis called across the stage. "Hey, Jen, the boys want to see you."

"What's up?" Jenny said, her gum-filled mouth slowing down to a talking speed.

Sammy frowned and wondered how many miles she got to a stick of gum and if she ever trapped any flies. "We were told that, when you were in the shop Monday, you went up the stairs to my room."

"That's a lie . . . I never . . . Okay, I walked up the stairs high enough to see your living room. Then I came back down. I thought your store was on two floors. That's all."

Brian stood tall, squinted, lowered his voice, and asked, "Was the desk in his room a light oak or a dark oak?"

Jenny stopped chomping her gum and gave Brian a deadpan look. Glancing back at Sammy, she asked, "Who told you that I went up the stairs and into your bedroom? I don't even know where your bedroom is."

"Somebody in the same room saw you go up."

"I can guess who it was. George Burk, right? Well, he's a liar."

Travis stepped forward. "You think it was Jenny who stole the money and then framed you? You're crazy. I know Jen, and she didn't do it."

"Look who's talking," Brian said.

Travis raised his hands and stepped back. "Hey, wait a minute. Do you think I'm in this too?"

"The robbers were a young girl and a young man," Sammy said. "In the store, you were talking to me in one room. It could have been a ploy to give Jenny time in the other room to sneak up the stairs and plant the money."

Travis motioned to the musical instruments. "Sammy, look at our broken-down equipment. Does it look like we suddenly came into a lot of money?"

Sammy raised his eyebrows. "A thief clever enough to pull an elaborate frame on Brian and me would know to sit on the money for a while."

"Clever? How clever can I be to have this second-rate band, exploiting the Amish culture?"

Sammy thought about Travis' words and nodded. "That makes sense, but let me advise you. If you are trying to look Amish, you shouldn't be wearing jewelry. And Jenny, your blond hair should be rolled and formed into a bun in the back. Also, Amish don't wear makeup."

Brian thought he should add something, so he said, "And the Amish don't smack their lips when they chew gum."

Travis smiled. "No, and the Amish don't advertise and perform in public, either." He glanced at the other band members. "We're just trying to give our band and our music an Amish flavor, that's all."

"If you pull it off," Sammy said, "you might be considered a clever young man." Sammy gave Jenny one last look. "Come on, Brian. We have to meet my parents at the car."

****

"I wanted to stay and hear the band," Brian said from the back seat of the car.

Mrs. Wilson turned her head to the back. "That's hard on the eardrums. The band noise and the erratic sounds of all the rides and the crowd would prevent you from hearing me now."

"Which might be a good idea," Brian joked.

"How did it go, boys?" Mr. Wilson asked into the rearview mirror. "Did you find out anything that will help you?"

Sammy leaned forward. "Nothing that will change anything. We still have four sets of suspects and one Lloyd Smedley."

"Who are the four sets of suspects?" Mrs. Wilson asked.

"We have Glen Clover and his cousin Angie Lowe, David Schultz and girlfriend Angie Lowe, George Burk and his sister, and Travis Wells and Jenny Herr."

"We have a bunch of suspects, but we have no evidence and no clues," Brian said.

"Ah, but we do have a clue, Brian," Sammy said.

"What clue?"

"The wigs, Brian, the wigs. They tell me in which direction to look. Now we have to prove it."

"And how are we going to do that?"

Sammy thought awhile then said, "We prove it by drawing the moth to the flame."

CHAPTER EIGHTEEN

David Schultz entered the Bird-in-Hand Country Store and glanced around. Only two people besides him were in the shop. A middle-aged man was talking to Mr. Wilson at the checkout counter.

Mr. Wilson looked at David and asked, "What can I do for you?"

"Sammy said he had a free baseball card for me."

"Oh, yes," Mr. Wilson said, looking around on the counter. "It's here somewhere."

"I have to leave," the older man said. "Check your paper money. If you find any of the red seals, give me a call." He threw his business card on the counter. "I'm paying $5,000 for each one."

"What was that about?" David asked after the front door closed.

Mr. Wilson opened the cash register. "Wait, I'm going to take a look." He slipped the paper money from their slots and examined each one.

"What are you looking for?" David asked.

"Red seals. See here?" Mr. Wilson said, indicating the right side of a twenty-dollar bill. "During the Korean Conflict, the mint started to print red seals on certain bills to honor the fighting men in the war. There won't be any seals on this bill because it isn't old enough." He examined the other bills, shook his head, and then returned them to the drawer.

"I'll have to tell my father," David said. "He has some old bills at home."

Mr. Wilson fumbled through some papers. "Here's your card. It's a Ken Griffy."

"It's not his rookie card, but I'll take it. Sammy said it's free."

Mr. Wilson smiled. "My son said there's no charge. That sounds like it's free to me."

"Okay, thanks, Mr. Wilson," David said and hurried out the door.

Sammy snuck in from the back room. "Now all we have to do is wait for the next one."

"Where's Brian?" Mr. Wilson asked.

"You know the binoculars that were sent to me? They were paid for with money orders from the Turkey Hill Market. Brian's checking with the clerks to see if they remember who bought them. He should be back soon."

"It sounds like a good lead," Mr. Wilson said.

Sammy's eyebrows lifted. "Only if the person wasn't wearing his hairy face disguise."

"Yeah," Sammy's father said, "that would kill a good lead."

The middle-aged man reentered the shop. "What time is the next suspect due in?" he asked.

Sammy checked his list and then his watch. "George Burk should arrive in about fifteen minutes, and you can repeat your performance. After that, it's Glen Clover and then Travis Wells. Why don't you come into the back room and have some coffee while we wait?"

Mr. Wilson reached under the counter and felt the book underneath. "I have the old book ready that you promised George."

****

Another phone call arrived.

Sammy, with Brian at his side, took a deep breath and answered it. "Hello."

"Sammy, this is Stan. You were right. I followed him to a barn along Church Road."

Sammy's plan was for the suspects to hear the fake story about red seals on certain bills. Knowing that most of Amos King's money would be old, the guilty person would then race to the stolen money to check it out. His mother, Uncle Stan, and two friends kept an eye on each suspect after he left the store.

"I heard from two other drivers so far," Sammy said. "They had nothing positive to report about the ones they followed. Your information sounds about right. Where exactly are you on Church Road?"

Stan gave him the directions and said he'd wait for the boys to arrive.

Brian's visit to Turkey Hill confirmed Sammy's suspicion. The hairy man had struck again. But, now, events were taking a turn for the good. If things went as planned, Sammy would expose the thieves and recover the money.

Half an hour later, Mr. Wilson dropped the boys off at the waiting car. "I'll drive away and then come back and wait for you," he said. "Please be careful."

Sammy and Brian waved as Mr. Wilson pulled away and then hurried over to Stan's car.

"How long has he been in there?" Sammy asked.

"About 45 minutes." He pointed and said, "His car is over there. Do you want me to come with you?"

"No, but thanks for your help. My father will be back. Call me tomorrow, and I'll tell you what happens."

The red barn was a smaller structure set apart from a larger barn. The name on the mailbox was Alex Hoffman. The electric wires headed for the house told Sammy the owner was non-Amish.

None of the suspects was named Hoffman. *Maybe a relative,* Sammy thought, as Brian and he neared the barn.

"Oh, boy, I can see the cell bars fading fast," Brian said, breaking away into a trot.

Sammy seized Brian by the back of his belt. "Hey, easy. We have to catch him with the money, so be quiet. He can't know that we're here."

Unfazed by his friend's sermon, Brian said, "The windows are covered over. We'll have to bust in."

"We can't do that," Sammy said. "This is private property."

"Don't worry. I'll catch him with the money. And if he tries anything funny, I'll . . ." Brian went into his judo chopping stance, his stiff open hands hacking the air. "I'll surround him and force him to the ground. Don't worry, Sammy. I'll try not to draw blood."

Sammy grabbed one of Brian's flailing arms and said, "Brian, stop that. Here's what we're going to do. We can't break in without a search warrant. If we can see that the stolen money is in there, we'll tell Detective Phillips, and he'll get a search warrant. Then we can go into the barn. But right now, we must find a way to see inside. Please be quiet."

The amateur detectives conducted a reconnaissance around the barn. Burlap covered the few windows. The large swinging barn doors were closed and latched. Any cracks between the boards gave useless thin slices of inside.

Brian dropped to his knees and utilized the two-inch gap under the doors. He saw a pair of legs standing at a table. He glanced up and whispered to Sammy. "I see him. He's in there."

"What's he doing?" Sammy asked, kneeling.

"You can't tell. It's dark. All you can see are his legs over there to the right."

As Sammy's eyes adjusted to the darkness, he saw the legs—coming their way. He snapped back. His heart was beating rapidly. His breathing deepened. "Quick, Brian, he's coming out."

The boys ran to the far side of the barn, away from the car.

One door swung open, closed, and then was padlocked. The young man headed for his car, apparently unaware of his audience.

The boys waited until the car disappeared before anything was said.

"That was a big bunch of nothing," Brian said. "Now what?"

Sammy put his hands into his pockets and walked toward his father's car, parked further down the road. Brian followed.

"Of all the suspects, he's the only one who did anything suspicious after hearing about the red seal," Sammy said. "Even if we suspect that the money is in the barn, we can't do anything."

Brian ran in front of Sammy and faced him, causing his friend to stop. "Do you know what I'm thinking, Sammy? You don't need a barn to hide the money. You can hide it in a wooden box. Like a box that was just painted and had a lid attached to it. Don't you see, Sammy? If a suspect is followed home, you don't know what he's doing behind closed doors."

Sammy started walking again. "You mean, we don't know what he's doing behind closed *garage* doors."

"Yeah, that's pretty profound. Right, Sammy?"

His partner's comment made Sammy think of baseball card boxes and how easy it would be to hide the money among boxed cards stacked on a shelf somewhere. He turned and glanced back at the barn.

He felt this was one test paper on which he wouldn't receive an A+.

"We can settle this right here," Brian said. "How about if I accidentally fall through one of those barn windows?"

"Brian, we don't know for certain where the money is. Do you want to be arrested again, this time for breaking and entering?" Sammy asked.

Brian kicked at a lump of dirt. "So what happens now?"

"I don't know, Brian. I just don't know where we go from here."

"I know where we go from here," Brian said with a sour face.

"Where?" Sammy asked.

"Jail. We go straight to jail."

A van passed Mr. Wilson's parked car and headed toward the teenagers. The driver's side window was down. The black object the driver held was aimed at the boys. He took two shots as he drove past them and continued down the road. He smiled. Those two shots plus the others he took with his camera would please his partner.

CHAPTER NINETEEN

Brian's eyes followed the longest crack in the ceiling. "Sammy, your house has 85 more years before it falls down."

"How do you know?" Sammy asked, continuing to work at his computer.

"You know how the lines in your palm can tell how long you have to live? The lines in your ceiling tell me this house has a life expectancy of 85 more years."

Sammy shrugged off Brian's lament with, "That's nice to know. Thank you, Brian. I'll make it a point not to be here 85 years from now."

Brian raised himself on his elbows. "Do I hear a hint of sarcasm in those words?"

"Brian, I realize you're trying to take my mind off of our troubles with your humor, but can you save it for another day?"

"Okay, but be forewarned. In 85 years, we'll be 100 years old. Even with our walkers, we may not be able to escape the collapse of the house."

Sammy stopped and gave Brian his cut-it-out stare.

"Okay, okay," Brian said, "but I still say that man took a picture of us from his car."

"Tourists do that all the time. They see barns, and they snap away."

"Maybe the man thought we were Amish. We do need haircuts."

Before he could reply, Sammy detected footsteps coming up the stairs. He glanced at the door, expecting someone to eventually enter the room. Instead, an envelope emerged under the door.

A soft knock was heard.

"Sammy, you have mail," Mrs. Wilson said. "I slid it under the door." Her footsteps descended the stairway.

"Okay, thanks, mom!" Sammy yelled.

Brian jumped from the bed and snatched up the envelope.

Sammy watched from his desk as Brian stood tall and sniffed the mail. "It could be one of those letter bombs," he said.

"What does it say on the envelope, Brian?"

"It says Sammy Wilson—"

Sammy interrupted Brian by sticking out his hand. "That's me, Brian. Give me my letter."

"I was just trying to intercept and discharge any danger that may come your way. But if you insist, here." Brian handed over the letter and moved behind his friend.

Sammy swiveled around and looked up at Brian.

"What are you doing? This could be for 'my eyes only' from the President."

"Oh, brother," Brian said, as he returned to the bed and bounced up and down. "Well, go ahead, open it."

Sammy opened the envelope and read the letter.

Sammy and Brian,
You won't find fingerprints so don't bother looking. I am giving you a sporting chance to find the real thieves of Amos King's money. You will find the guilty person if you search these locations.

    town clock
    The Cloister
    Oyster Point Family Health Center
    Louis Family Restaurant
    mud sale
    Haydn Zug's

Sammy checked the return address. There was none. He threw the letter onto the desk. "Here, Brian. What do you make of this?"

Brian hurried to the desk and picked up the letter. "Are you sure the President wants me to see it?"

Sammy raised his eyebrows and tilted his head. "Somebody does. Read it."

Brian did. "I bet more bundles of money are hidden at these places, and they want us to get caught with them."

Sammy took the letter back from Brian. He checked the envelope again. The letter was mailed in Bird-in-Hand. All lettering was done on a computer. He reread the letter looking for clues and found none.

"I can't believe these people want us to catch them. They're throwing a puzzle at us and daring us to solve it. It doesn't make sense. One thing we know— we can't trust them."

Brian scratched his head. "Do they expect us to go to all the places on the list?"

"We are not going down that road again," Sammy said, studying the list. Then he scanned the letter into his computer for insurance and gave the original back to Brian. "Okay, Brian, let's see if we can outsmart them. What do these places have in common?"

"Two of them are restaurants, food. One tells the time. One is a tourist attraction. One has doctors and nurses, and one has mud. I don't see any one thing they have in common," Brian said as he studied the monitor.

"I don't either," Sammy said. "Four of them are proper nouns. Two are common nouns."

"I know where four of them are. The Cloister is in Ephrata. The Oyster Point Health Center is on the Marietta Pike. Louis Restaurant is on the Marietta Pike in Rohrerstown. Haydn Zug's is a restaurant in East Petersburg." Brian shrugged. "How do they expect us to search the town clock and a mud sale? Where are they?"

"Landisville has a town clock," Sammy said. "They raised money to repair it. Mud sales are outdoor auctions held by various fire companies in March and April during the summer thaw and rainy season. That's why they're called mud sales."

The list looked like an unsolvable mess to Brian. "I say we ignore it. Don't play their game. That way we can stay out of trouble."

Sammy brushed the hair back from his eyes. "They already have us framed for the robbery. What more can they want?"

Brian hopped on the bed, reclined back, and studied the ceiling. He held the letter up in front of his face and stared at the word clock. After twenty seconds, he took the letter away and focused at a spot on the ceiling. He saw the black words as white on the ceiling. "Hey, I know. This is like the pictures on the quilt. The pictures form words."

"These are words not pictures," Sammy said.

Brian sat up. "But that's the idea. We reverse the words into pictures."

"Where do we go from there?" Sammy asked, giving Brian the opportunity to think through his idea.

Brian thought for a moment. "Well, then each picture represents a word."

"It's worth a try," Sammy said. "Let's do it. Visualize a town clock. What word do you get from it?"

"Time. T for time." Brian said it like *what else could it be?*

Sammy wrote a T on scrap paper. "Okay, next, The Cloister."

"That's easy, religion. R for religion."

Sammy wrote an R and a C. "Could be C for commune. The Cloister was a religious communal group where people lived together, sharing the chores."

Brian's voice got louder to override Sammy's additional comments. "The health center could be D for doctor, or S for sickness."

Sammy jotted down the letters.

"F for food at the restaurant," Brian continued.

"I'm going to add C for cook," Sammy said.

Brian was already thinking about mud sale. "Mud sale is A for auction. Right, Sammy?" he finally said.

Sammy wrote the A, and then said, "Haydn Zug's is a restaurant. Are we going for an F for food and a C for cook again?"

"Yeah, okay," Brian said. "Now what does that give us? Does it spell anything?"

Sammy studied the letters he had written.

T R(C) D(S) F(C) A F(C)

"I don't see anything close to a word anywhere here. Try something different. What do we see when we visualize the name? For example the town clock is round, so we have an R for round. It could also be N for numbers."

Brian bounced on the bed. "Oh, I get it. When I visualize The Cloister, I see buildings. So B for buildings."

"Right," Sammy said, "and the health center would be . . . what?"

The bed stopped shaking as Brian closed his eyes. "I see a building, doctors in their small examination rooms. I see sick people. I see . . . I see this is not working."

"You're right," Sammy said and slammed his pen down on the desk. He brought his hands to his face and leaned back. This caper was going nowhere. He needed a handle to grasp. He needed to be in charge. He needed puzzle pieces. He felt helpless, like a student driver with the car driving him instead of him driving the car. The walls were closing in. He was in jail, and the trial hadn't even started.

Brian stood at the bed. He knew better then to disturb Sammy's emotional state. Any attempt at humor would be wasted energy. Holding the letter in his left hand, Brian eased himself over to the desk.

Sammy heard the motion and slid his hands from his face. "What are you doing?"

"I want to use the computer to go on the Internet."

Sammy slid his chair back, allowing Brian access to the computer.

Using the Google search engine, Brian typed in: Landisville PA town clock. Many listings came up, most having nothing to do with the Landisville clock. He read them, and at the bottom was an entry for the Gap town clock. "We forgot the most famous town clock in the area," he said to Sammy. "It's a tourist attraction." He twisted around and waited for Sammy to answer.

"The one at Gap," Sammy said finally. "It's the one we see when we go to the shore."

"Right on," Brian said.

Sammy pushed Brian aside and picked up the letter Brian had laid on the desk. He read the last sentence: You will find the guilty person if you search these locations. He glanced at each listing. "Gordonville is probably the largest and most popular mud sale in the area."

Brian knew his friend was on to something. "I believe it is. Why?"

Sammy breathed deeply and smiled. "We just got a free pass from jail. I was right all along, and this letter confirms it."

"Who does the letter say did it, and how are you going to prove it?"

"Not now, Brian. Now, these two little pigs are going to market."

CHAPTER TWENTY

That afternoon, Sammy explained his red seal con game and its results to Detective Phillips. He gave the detective a list of the people who had access to his bedroom to plant the stolen money. He laid out reasons for his suspicions, produced the anonymous letter, and explained its solution. Sammy thought he knew who had sent the letter, but he didn't know why. What captured Phillips' attention was Sammy's plan to prove himself right.

By 10:00 the next morning, the reception area at the police station was filling with suspects. David Schultz and Angie Lowe, George Burk and his sister Amy, and Travis Wells and Jenny Herr were there. They were waiting for Lloyd Smedley and Glen Clover.

Smedley and Glen wandered in at 10:10. Only Smedley said that he was sorry he was late.

A side door opened, and Detective Phillips appeared. "Follow me, please," he said. The hallway was long and ended at a large interrogation room.

When everyone was seated around the rectangular table, Sammy and Brian entered the room.

Detective Phillips stood at the head of the table. "I believe you all know Sammy Wilson and Brian Helm. They have been arrested for what the media now calls 'the buggy heist.' They claim that they were framed. Of course, the evidence says otherwise. They think that one of you did it."

David squirmed in his chair, causing Angie to elbow him and say, "Sit still."

Detective Phillips continued. "In order to prove them guilty, I want you all to take a test to show you are innocent." Phillips called across the hall. "Detective Wetzel, will you have the money from the evidence locker brought in?"

Travis shoved his chair backward. "Is this going to take long? I have a schedule to keep."

Phillips held out his hand and locked eyes with the musician. "Not long."

Travis inched his chair back to the table.

Seconds later, a patrolman carried a tray of bundled money into the room.

"Put it on the table, please," Phillips said, eyeing the money. "Hey, I only wanted the money from the buggy heist. You also have what looks like the drug money we confiscated yesterday."

The patrolman gave Phillips a strange look. "Detective Wetzel said to bring the tray of money to you. Do you want me to take it back?"

Phillips looked displeased but said, "No, that's okay. Thank you."

Sammy and Brian remained quiet, standing against the wall. Sammy wanted this to be Detective Phillips' show, and indeed, he was doing well.

Phillips started his prepared speech. "We took oil and dust residue off the stolen money and broke it down into its elements. From that, we developed a pattern analysis." Phillips opened a case on the side table. He took out cotton swabs and a bottle of liquid. "If you are right-handed, put your right hand on the table. If you are left-handed, put your left hand on the table. I am going to take a specimen of residue from your fingers. If your fingers recently touched the stolen money, we will know."

Several suspects were hesitant about making their hands available. Others had to decide which was the right hand and which was the left. Smedley wiped his hands on his jeans before submitting to the request.

Phillips took his time, collecting samples, labeling each swab, and placing them into sealed containers. When he was finished, he breathed deeply and said, "I'll know the results tomorrow."

Throughout this process, the money stayed displayed on the table.

"Can we go now?" Travis asked anxiously.

"No, everyone stay here until I come back," Detective Phillips said and picked up the case in one hand and the swab samples in the other. With his hands full, he faced the seated group and said, "Oh, will someone bring just the buggy-heist money to my office?"

Two hands snatched the money from the table.

Sammy smiled and coughed. Detective Phillips turned around and saw George Burk standing and holding the money.

The others in the room noticed that Sammy, Brian, and Detective Phillips were quietly looking at George. They, too, glanced at George, wondering what the attraction was. The room got still and quiet as an uneasy atmosphere developed.

"What?" George said, seeing the attention focused on him. "I'm not stealing the money. I'm taking it to your office like you said."

"Of all the packs of money on the table, how did you know which were from the buggy heist?" Phillips asked with concern.

"That's why I didn't help," David Schultz said. "I didn't know which bundles to get."

Jenny Herr raised her hand. "Me, too," she said.

Phillips repeated, "Well, George, how did you know which bundles to get from the tray?"

George extended his hands to better display the money. "Because of the rubber bands. The other bundles have paper bands. Doesn't Amos King's money have rubber bands around them?"

"How did you know that?" Phillips asked. "That was one bit of information we withheld from the media. Only the people who stole the money would know about the rubber bands."

George dropped his arms and plopped the money back onto the tray. "I must have heard it from someone."

Phillips shook his head. "That won't do, George. Only a few of us knew."

"It was a lucky guess," George said after he swallowed hard. His face was pale, and perspiration was forming on his upper lip.

The detective placed the case and swab samples on the table. "These swab test results that come back tomorrow won't be a lucky guess. Will they show that you and Amy touched Amos King's money?"

Amy stood and pounded her fists on George's chest. "You lied to me. You said we wouldn't be caught."

Sammy had heard that line before, and it made him wince. He spoke out for the first time. "Amy, you don't commit a crime because you might be caught," he said bluntly. "The reason you don't commit a crime is that it's morally wrong."

Detective Phillips placed George and Amy under arrest and read them their rights while cuffing their hands behind them. He dismissed the others from the room except for Lloyd Smedley. Sammy had one more item to discuss.

Unexpectedly, Sammy asked, "George and Amy, you're related to Lloyd Smedley, aren't you?"

Amy's face was glum. "We don't advertise the fact," Amy said. "Sure, he's our stepfather. He's some father, huh? He's a thief."

Smedley glanced up from the table. "And now, so are you and George," Smedley said sadly.

George butted his body against the table, pushing it against his stepfather sitting on the other side. "Yeah, we're a chip off the old block," he said.

Smedley shoved the table away from his body. "I'm not your real father. You're not no chip off of my block."

Phillips forced George to sit back into his chair.

"What I don't understand," Sammy said, "is, if you two hate your stepfather so much, why attack me and say to stay away from him?"

"He is supposed to be our father. He stepped in when our real father abandoned us eight years ago. And, anyway, you continued to hound him. You and Brian had him arrested for attempting to steal Amos King's money. You set him up. You framed him."

Sammy remained calm, knowing that George's answer to the next question would cause a dismissal of the charges against Brian and him. "Is that the reason you stole the money from the buggy and then framed Brian and me?"

"Do you want to know the real reason I stole the money?" George said defiantly, his face red. "I'll tell you." George pointed to Sammy. "It was because of you. You had my stepfather arrested. He promised me money so I could start my own antique business. When he tried to get the money, you and Brian stopped him."

"Did you ever think, George, that the reason your stepfather tried to steal the money was to get you started in the antique business?"

"Look, he owed me. He made me work at the flea market for years."

"And making duplicate keys was one of your jobs, wasn't it?" Sammy said.

"That's right," George said, trying to get sympathy.

"Is that when you made a copy of Glen Clover's car key?"

George's face relaxed, and in a bragging tone, he said, "Sure, why not? I told him the first cut was bad, and I kept it for myself. What's wrong with that? So I take a girl for a joy ride once in a while when I see Glen's car in his driveway. Big deal. My stepfather wouldn't buy me no car. I didn't have nothing." He nodded his head at his stepfather. "That was his fault."

"Is anything your fault?" Sammy asked, and then waited for that to sink in. "Your stepfather is going to jail because of you. You demanded money from him—money he didn't have. You forced your stepfather to step over the line and break the law. I hate to say this, but I don't think you care about your stepfather at all."

"Okay, okay, I wanted to show him I was better than him!" George shouted. "What's wrong with that?" George took a deep breath and glanced at his stepfather. "You were always telling me what to do. You said I was dumb. Well, I showed you, didn't I? I did what you couldn't do. I stole the money. It was easy, taking money from an old lady. She had the money in a paper bag, thousands of dollars in a lousy three-cent grocery bag."

Phillips squeezed George's shoulder as he half stood and rattled the handcuffs that restrained him from behind. "Simmer down, George. Things will go easier for you if you relax and cooperate."

"Yeah, okay, I planned the whole thing—the robbery and setting you boys up to take the blame." He sat back and smiled. "Not bad for someone who only went to the eighth grade. I planned the whole thing. Well, my sister helped me."

Sammy said, "Your sister's the girl my mother directed to the restroom downstairs, so you could get to my bedroom upstairs."

"Smart, huh?" George said. "I knew a nerdy softy like you would allow me to use the bathroom upstairs in your apartment. It was easy to enter your bedroom and stash the money under your bed."

"It was easy for your mother to become Mrs. Thomas, too," Sammy said. "She used to do acting in the local theaters, didn't she? I believe her last acting job was playing the role of Mrs. Betty Thomas."

Sammy's comment disturbed George. "You keep my mother out of this. She didn't know about the money. I told her I was playing a joke on you and Brian. Playing the role of Mrs. Thomas was only a performance for her. Please leave her out of this," George pleaded. "She's suffered enough, having Lloyd as her husband."

Phillips pulled up on George's arm and glanced at Amy, who sat quietly beside her brother. "Okay, you two, let's go and get you booked."

"Sport, you and Brian did it again," Smedley said after they were alone in the room. He looked at the floor. "I'm sorry my son and daughter got into this mess. I thought they might learn from my mistakes."

Sammy pulled out a chair and sat next to Smedley. "It was you who sent me the letter, wasn't it?" he asked.

Smedley paused, then looked up. "After you asked me about making a key for Glen Clover, I remembered that George could have made it. When I got home that evening, and talked to him, he admitted he made a copy of the key for himself and had stolen the money." Smedley snapped his fingers. "Just like that, like he was proud of it. I knew he'd be caught." He sighed. "In time, we all get caught." Smedley stood. "How'd you know it was me who sent the letter?"

"You're the only person I know who likes to use the word sport. In the letter, you wanted to give us a 'sporting' chance to catch the thieves."

"Ain't that kind of a long shot?"

"It's the only hope I had, until you just confirmed it."

Smedley patted Sammy's shoulder and said, "Thanks for not telling my son and daughter about the letter. The sooner they pay for what they did, the better off they are." With shoulders stooped, Smedley plodded past the boys to the door and in seconds was gone.

Brian slipped the letter from his pocket and spread it on the table. "Okay, now, explain this to me. How did you get the name George from this list?"

Sammy took a pen from his pocket and made notations on the letter. He stood back and allowed Brian to examine it.

Sammy and Brian,

You won't find fingerprints so don't bother looking. I am giving you a sporting chance to find the real thieves of Amos King's money. You will find the guilty person if you search these <u>locations</u>.

town clock _Gap_

The Cloister _Ephrata_

Oyster Point Family Health Center _Oyster Point_

Louis Family Restaurant _Rohrerstown_

mud sale _Gordonville_

Haydn Zug's _East Petersburg_

"When you mentioned the town clock at Gap, my eye went to the word locations. That was the key to arriving at the name of the thief. When you write the location of each item, its first letter spells out the name."

Brian looked at each letter that Sammy had underlined. "George. They spell George."

Sammy continued. "Do you remember when I said that the wigs were a clue in this case?"

"Yeah. What did that mean?"

"If you're a blond and you want to disguise yourself with a wig, what color would you choose?"

"A dark one, black or brown," Brian said.

"And if your hair was dark what color would you pick?"

Brian had the idea. "Blond."

"Correct," Sammy said. "The only dark-haired girl among the suspects was Amy. Thus, her brother

George was a good candidate for the young male. When I arranged for the red seal flimflam, George was the one who immediately went to the barn supposedly to examine the stolen money. That strengthened my belief that George was the prime suspect. This letter was the final clue that pointed to George."

"How did you connect George and Amy to Lloyd Smedley?"

"Yesterday, when we went back to the flea market, I wanted to get a better look at the family photo that Smedley had at his counter. Even though it was an old picture, I saw the resemblance between George and Amy and the children in the photo."

"But those things, pointing to George, only created suspicions. Now I had to prove it, especially if we wanted a judge to issue a search warrant for the barn."

Detective Phillips wore a big smile as he walked into the room. "Your idea worked. This is exactly why we keep back details in a case. It establishes a connection to a crime of which the public is not aware. These are facts that only the guilty person would know. In this case, that the money was secured with rubber bands."

"Don't forget the sample residue you took from their fingers," Brian added.

Sammy and Phillips chuckled. "It doesn't mean a thing," Phillips said. "There is no such test as the pattern analysis test I described. From the time the thieves last touched the money, their hands contacted many things and were washed many times. The value of the swab test was to add weight to the guilt the thieves already felt. The more guilt they feel, the more they want to talk."

"We saw a good example of that today," Sammy said. "George Burk had a lot to get off his chest."

"Judge Ashworth is issuing a search warrant now," Phillips said. "I suspect we'll find the money and the wigs in the barn. I'm sorry I had to arrest you and Brian, but my hands were tied. I do want you to know that I had assigned an officer to follow you boys to take pictures and to assist you, had you needed help."

"See, Sammy, I told you," Brian said.

"Was the officer to assist us or to get more evidence against us?" Sammy asked.

Detective Phillips smiled, picked up the tray of bundled money, and walked out of the room.

Brian moped over to a chair and slumped down. His head rested on his arms folded on the table. "I'm tired. Solving this case sapped my energy. My mind is overworked. I think we should stop at Coleman's and get some ice cream." He looked up at Sammy with a pitiful expression.

Cleared of all charges brought against them, Sammy relaxed and was ready to join Brian's unpredictable world. In a kidding mood, he said, "We don't have time for ice cream, Brian. We have to prepare for our next case."

Brian frowned. "What case?"

With a serious face, Sammy said, "Amos King's money still has to get from the barn to the police station."

"So?"

Sammy headed for the door. "Don't you see, Brian? A police car must transport the money from the barn to the police station."

"Oh, yeah, that's right." Brian raised his arm, a finger pointing straight up. "That makes our next case *The Police Car Heist.*"

Sammy smiled and said, "That's a thought. In the meantime, let's go get some ice cream."

"I want chocolate," Brian said, gathering energy to spring up from the chair and race after his friend out the door and down the hall. "Hey, wait up for me."

The End